NANCY DREW

AND THE CLUE CREW®

D0427933

"INTEResting iS WHAT MY DaD CaLLs aRt WHEN HE REaLLY tHinKS it StinKs" - NaNCY DREW

PAPERCUTZ™

POP ART PRODUCTIONS

NANCY DREW GRAPHIC NOVELS AVAILABLE FROM PAPERCUTZ

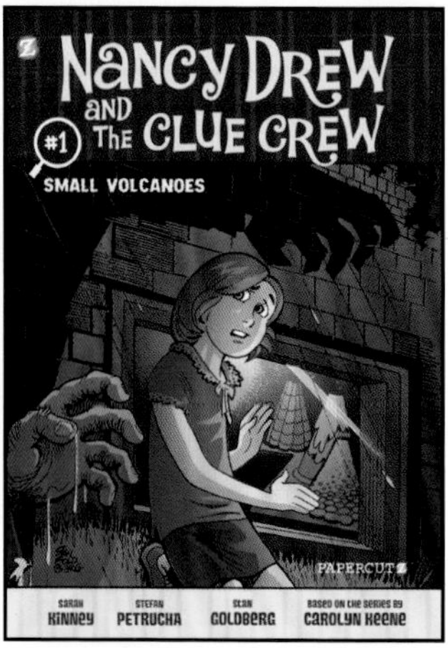
NANCY DREW AND THE CLUE CREW
#1
SMALL VOLCANOES
PAPERCUTZ
SARAH KINNEY
STEFAN PETRUCHA
STAN GOLDBERG
BASED ON THE SERIES BY CAROLYN KEENE

NANCY DREW AND THE CLUE CREW #1 "Small Volcanoes"

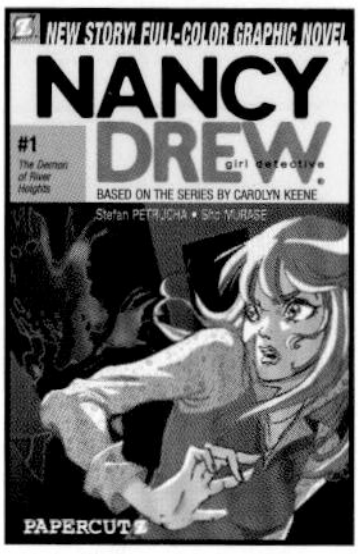
NEW STORY! FULL-COLOR GRAPHIC NOVEL
NANCY DREW
girl detective
#1
BASED ON THE SERIES BY CAROLYN KEENE
Stefan PETRUCHA • Sho MURASE
PAPERCUTZ

#1 "The Demon of River Heights"

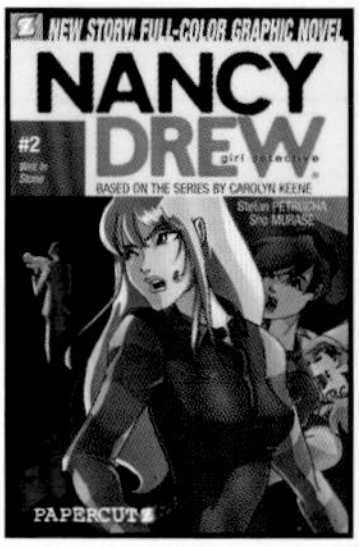
NEW STORY! FULL-COLOR GRAPHIC NOVEL
NANCY DREW
girl detective
#2
BASED ON THE SERIES BY CAROLYN KEENE
PAPERCUTZ

#2 "Writ In Stone"

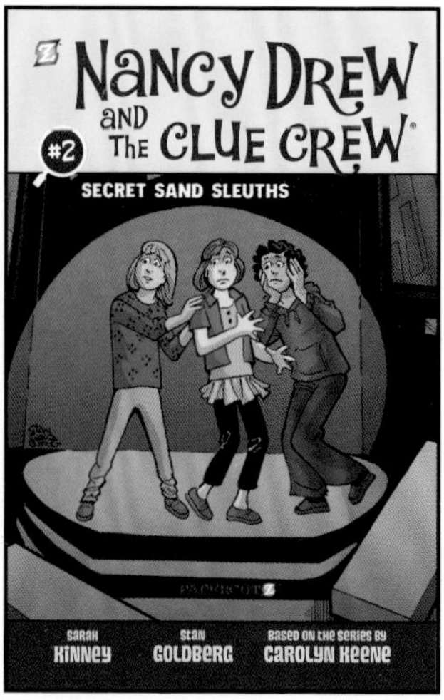
NANCY DREW AND THE CLUE CREW
#2
SECRET SAND SLEUTHS
PAPERCUTZ
SARAH KINNEY
STAN GOLDBERG
BASED ON THE SERIES BY CAROLYN KEENE

NANCY DREW AND THE CLUE CREW #2 "Secret Sand Sleuths"

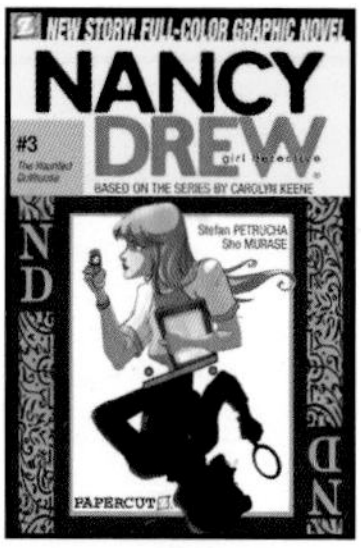
NEW STORY! FULL-COLOR GRAPHIC NOVEL
NANCY DREW
girl detective
#3
BASED ON THE SERIES BY CAROLYN KEENE
Stefan PETRUCHA
Sho MURASE
PAPERCUTZ

#3 "The Haunted Dollhouse"

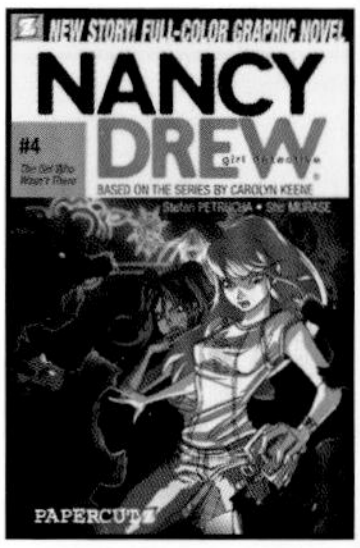
NEW STORY! FULL-COLOR GRAPHIC NOVEL
NANCY DREW
girl detective
#4
BASED ON THE SERIES BY CAROLYN KEENE
Stefan PETRUCHA • Sho MURASE
PAPERCUTZ

#4 "The Girl Who Wasn't There"

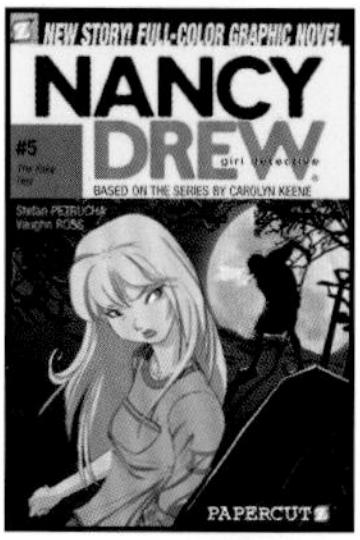
NEW STORY! FULL-COLOR GRAPHIC NOVEL
NANCY DREW
girl detective
#5
BASED ON THE SERIES BY CAROLYN KEENE
PAPERCUTZ

#5 "The Fake Heir"

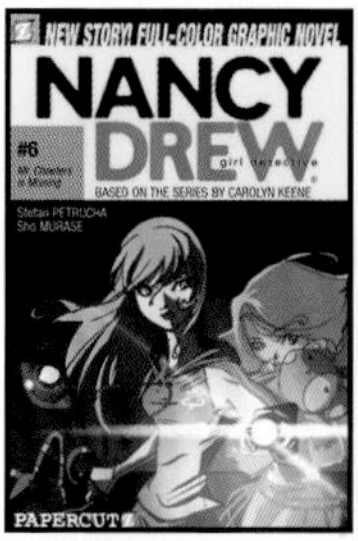
NEW STORY! FULL-COLOR GRAPHIC NOVEL
NANCY DREW
girl detective
#6
BASED ON THE SERIES BY CAROLYN KEENE
Stefan PETRUCHA
Sho MURASE
PAPERCUTZ

#6 "Mr. Cheeters Is Missing"

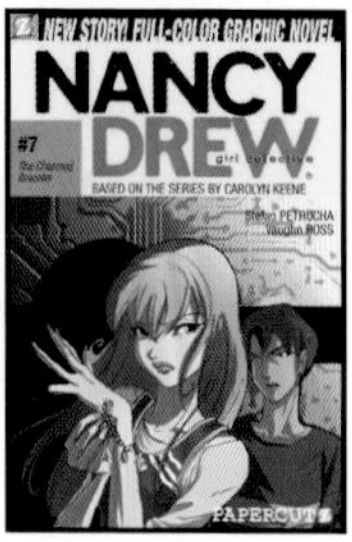
NEW STORY! FULL-COLOR GRAPHIC NOVEL
NANCY DREW
girl detective
#7
BASED ON THE SERIES BY CAROLYN KEENE
PAPERCUTZ

#7 "The Charmed Bracelet"

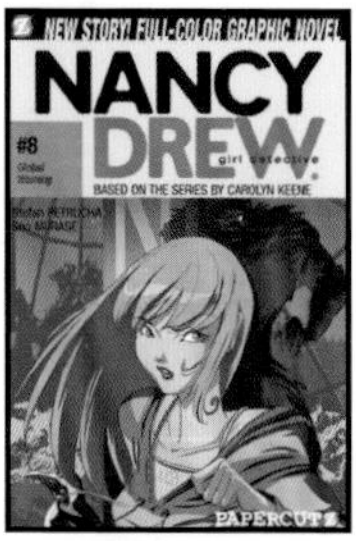
NEW STORY! FULL-COLOR GRAPHIC NOVEL
NANCY DREW
girl detective
#8
BASED ON THE SERIES BY CAROLYN KEENE
PAPERCUTZ

#8 "Global Warning"

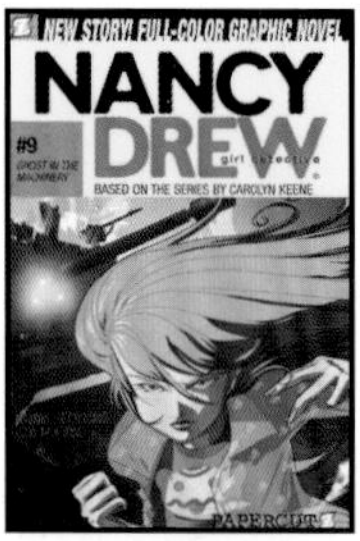
NEW STORY! FULL-COLOR GRAPHIC NOVEL
NANCY DREW
girl detective
#9
BASED ON THE SERIES BY CAROLYN KEENE
PAPERCUTZ

#9 "Ghost In The Machinery"

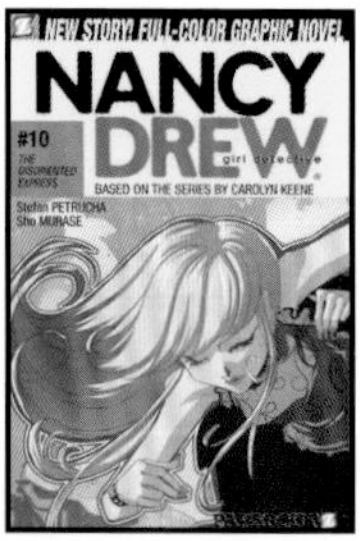
NEW STORY! FULL-COLOR GRAPHIC NOVEL
NANCY DREW
girl detective
#10
BASED ON THE SERIES BY CAROLYN KEENE
Stefan PETRUCHA
Sho MURASE

#10 "The Disoriented Express"

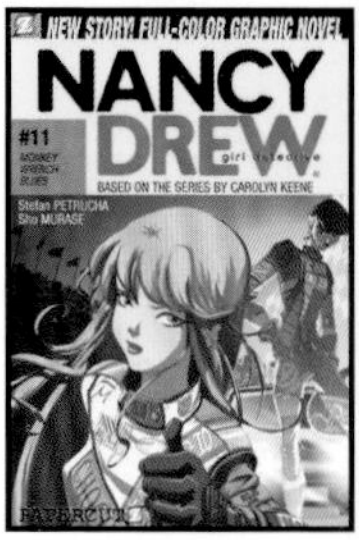
NEW STORY! FULL-COLOR GRAPHIC NOVEL
NANCY DREW
girl detective
#11
BASED ON THE SERIES BY CAROLYN KEENE
Stefan PETRUCHA
Sho MURASE
PAPERCUTZ

#11 "Monkey Wrench Blues"

See page 55 for more NANCY DREW graphic novels!

NANCY DREW graphic novels are available at booksellers everywhere.

NANCY DREW graphic novels are $7.95 each in paperback and $12.95 each in hardcover. NANCY DREW AND THE CLUE CREW graphic novels are $7.99 paperback and $11.99 hardcover each in hardcover. You can also order online at www.papercutz.com. Or call 1-800-886-1223, Monday through Fridays, 9 – 5 EST. MC, Visa, and AmEx accepted. To order by mail, please add $4.00 for postage and handling for first book ordered, $1.00 for each additional book and make check payable to NBM Publishing. Send to: Papercutz, 160 Broadway, Suite 700, East Wing, New York, NY 10038.

NANCY DREW and NANCY DREW AND THE CLUE CREW graphic novels are also available digitally wherever e-books are sold.

www.papercutz.com

NANCY DREW AND THE CLUE CREW

#2

SECRET SAND SLEUTHS

SARAH KINNEY - WRITER

STAN GOLDBERG - ARTIST

LAURIE E. SMITH - COLORIST

BASED ON THE SERIES BY CAROLYN KEENE

PAPERCUTZ™

NEW YORK

Nancy Drew and the Clue Crew
#2 "Secret Sand Sleuths"
Sarah Kinney – Writer
Stan Goldberg – Artist
Laurie E. Smith – Colorist
Tom Orzechowski – Letterer
Production by Nelson Design Group, LLC
Associate Editor – Michael Petranek
Jim Salicrup
Editor-in-Chief

ISBN: 978-1-59707-376-9 paperback edition
ISBN: 978-1-59707-377-6 hardcover edition

Printed in China
January 2013 by Asia One Printing, LTD
13/F Asia One Tower
8 Fung Yip St., Chaiwan, Hong Kong

Distributed by Macmillan

First Printing

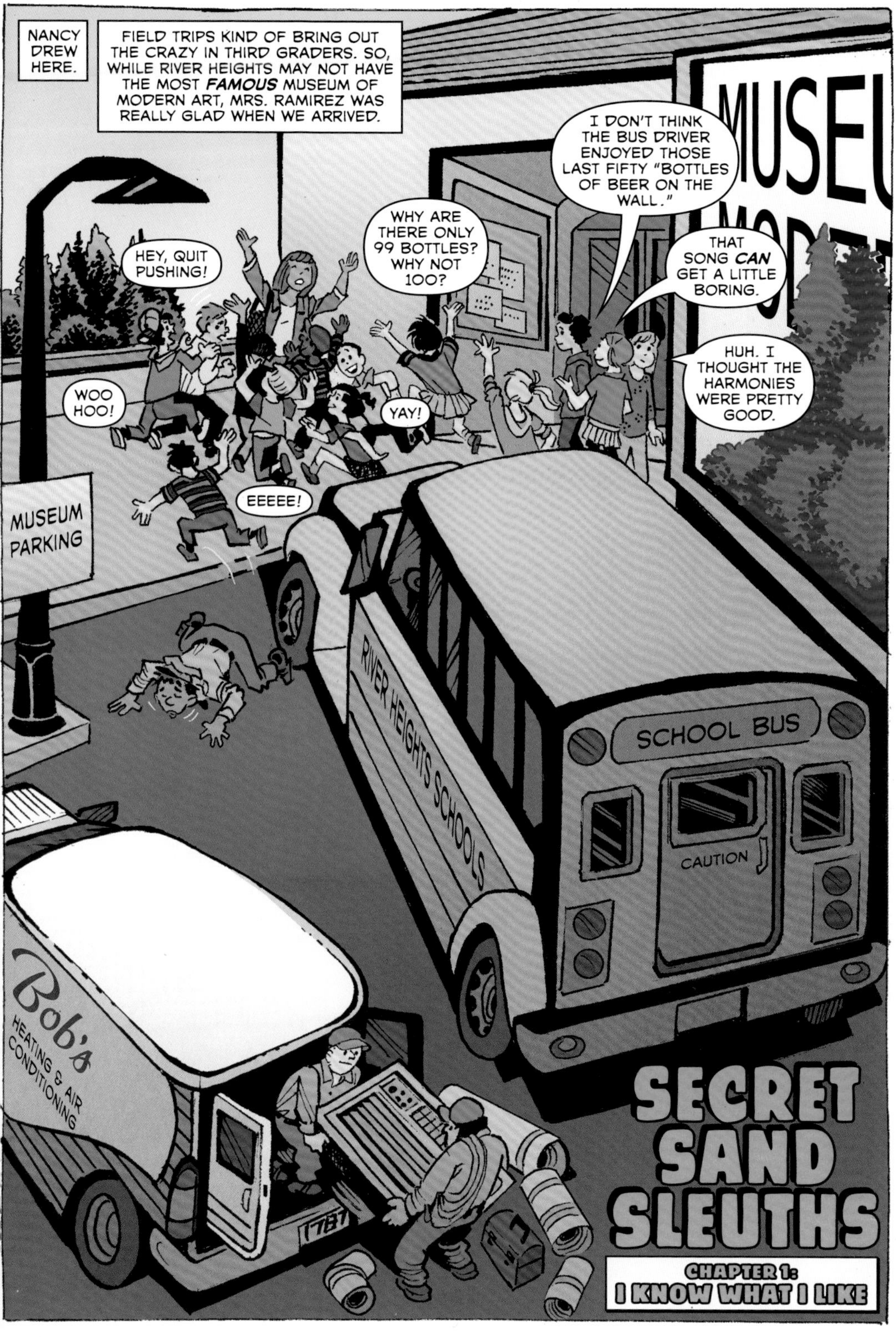
NANCY DREW HERE.
FIELD TRIPS KIND OF BRING OUT THE CRAZY IN THIRD GRADERS. SO, WHILE RIVER HEIGHTS MAY NOT HAVE THE MOST FAMOUS MUSEUM OF MODERN ART, MRS. RAMIREZ WAS REALLY GLAD WHEN WE ARRIVED.
MUSEU
HEY, QUIT PUSHING!
WHY ARE THERE ONLY 99 BOTTLES? WHY NOT 100?
I DON'T THINK THE BUS DRIVER ENJOYED THOSE LAST FIFTY "BOTTLES OF BEER ON THE WALL."
THAT SONG CAN GET A LITTLE BORING.
HUH. I THOUGHT THE HARMONIES WERE PRETTY GOOD.
WOO HOO!
YAY!
EEEEE!
MUSEUM PARKING
RIVER HEIGHTS SCHOOLS
SCHOOL BUS
CAUTION
Bob's HEATING & AIR CONDITIONING
1787
SECRET SAND SLEUTHS
CHAPTER 1: I KNOW WHAT I LIKE

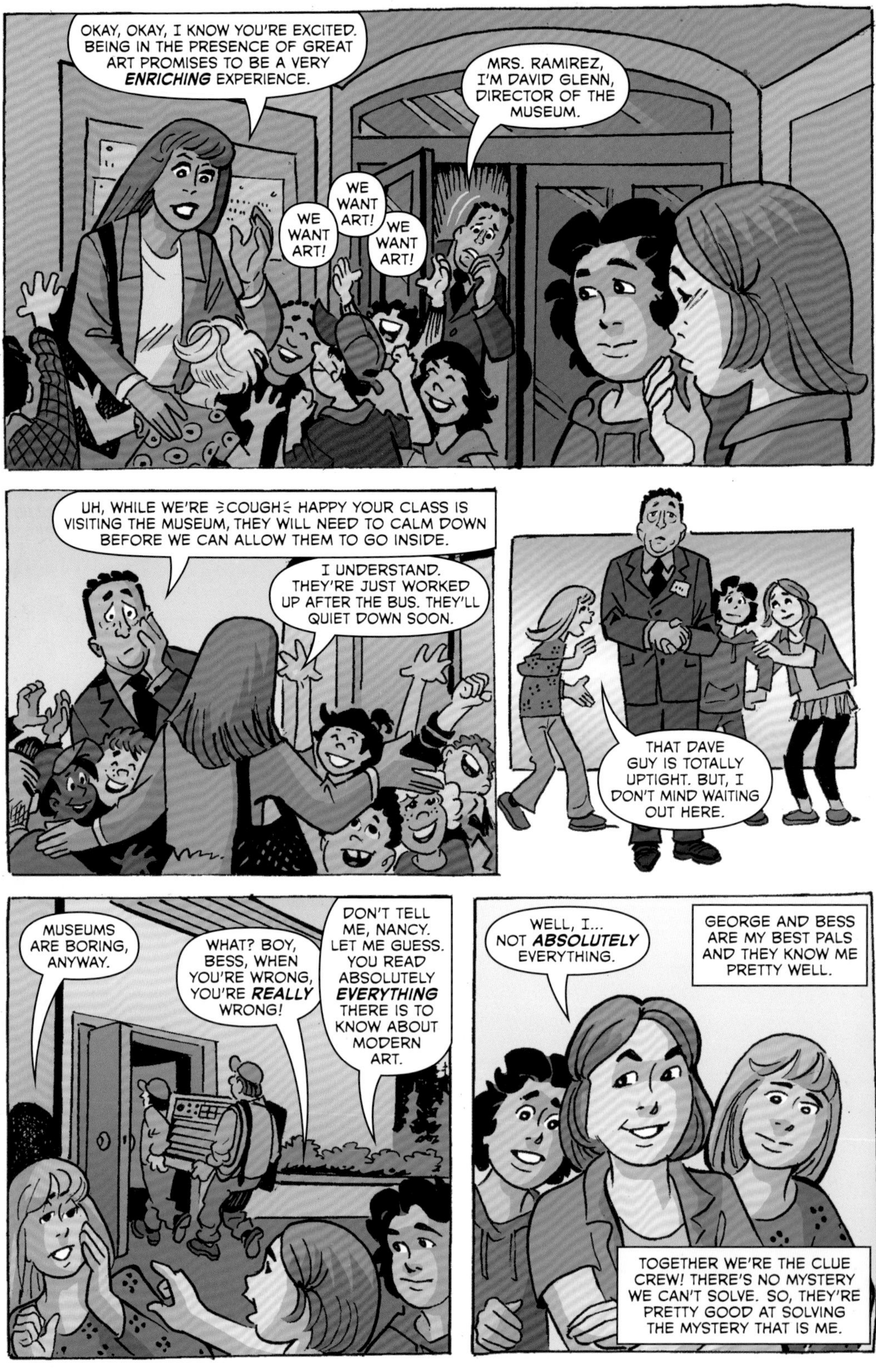
OKAY, OKAY, I KNOW YOU'RE EXCITED. BEING IN THE PRESENCE OF GREAT ART PROMISES TO BE A VERY ENRICHING EXPERIENCE.
WE WANT ART!
WE WANT ART!
WE WANT ART!
MRS. RAMIREZ, I'M DAVID GLENN, DIRECTOR OF THE MUSEUM.
UH, WHILE WE'RE *COUGH* HAPPY YOUR CLASS IS VISITING THE MUSEUM, THEY WILL NEED TO CALM DOWN BEFORE WE CAN ALLOW THEM TO GO INSIDE.
I UNDERSTAND. THEY'RE JUST WORKED UP AFTER THE BUS. THEY'LL QUIET DOWN SOON.
THAT DAVE GUY IS TOTALLY UPTIGHT. BUT, I DON'T MIND WAITING OUT HERE.
MUSEUMS ARE BORING, ANYWAY.
WHAT? BOY, BESS, WHEN YOU'RE WRONG, YOU'RE REALLY WRONG!
DON'T TELL ME, NANCY. LET ME GUESS. YOU READ ABSOLUTELY EVERYTHING THERE IS TO KNOW ABOUT MODERN ART.
WELL, I... NOT ABSOLUTELY EVERYTHING.
GEORGE AND BESS ARE MY BEST PALS AND THEY KNOW ME PRETTY WELL.
TOGETHER WE'RE THE CLUE CREW! THERE'S NO MYSTERY WE CAN'T SOLVE. SO, THEY'RE PRETTY GOOD AT SOLVING THE MYSTERY THAT IS ME.

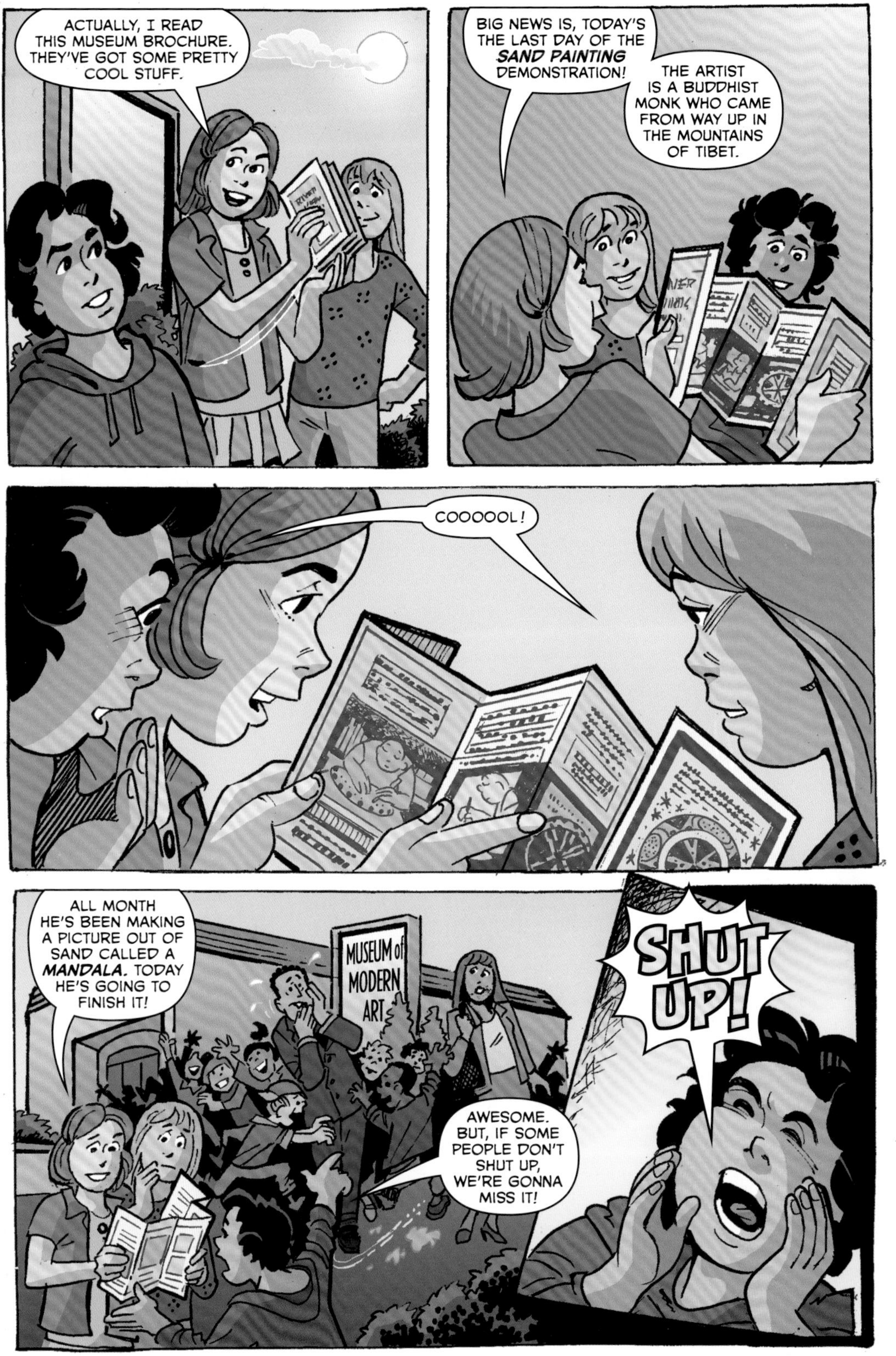
ACTUALLY, I READ THIS MUSEUM BROCHURE. THEY'VE GOT SOME PRETTY COOL STUFF.
BIG NEWS IS, TODAY'S THE LAST DAY OF THE ***SAND PAINTING*** DEMONSTRATION!
THE ARTIST IS A BUDDHIST MONK WHO CAME FROM WAY UP IN THE MOUNTAINS OF TIBET.
COOOOOL!
ALL MONTH HE'S BEEN MAKING A PICTURE OUT OF SAND CALLED A ***MANDALA.*** TODAY HE'S GOING TO FINISH IT!
MUSEUM of MODERN ART
AWESOME. BUT, IF SOME PEOPLE DON'T SHUT UP, WE'RE GONNA MISS IT!
SHUT UP!

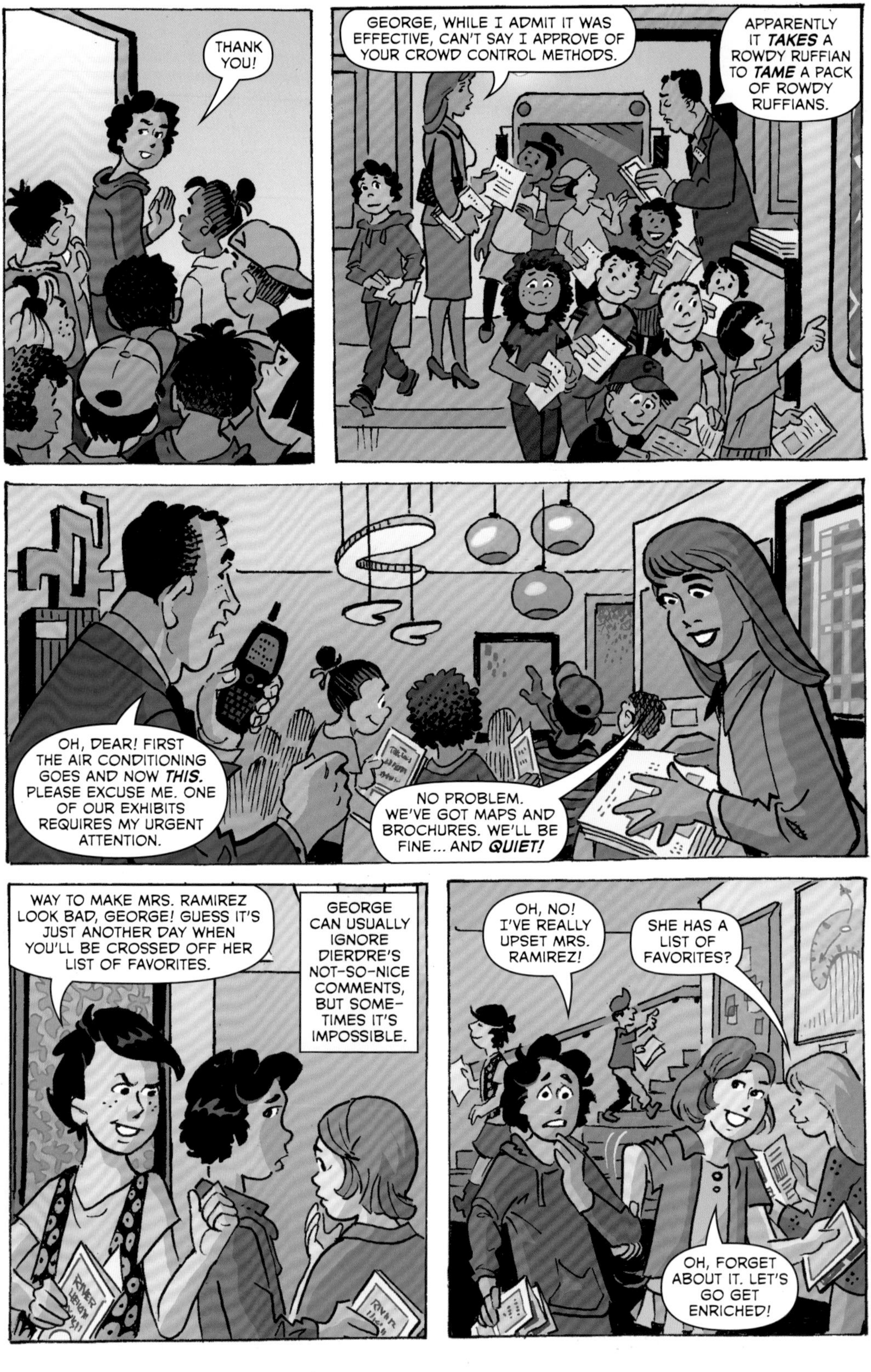
THANK YOU!
GEORGE, WHILE I ADMIT IT WAS EFFECTIVE, CAN'T SAY I APPROVE OF YOUR CROWD CONTROL METHODS.
APPARENTLY IT TAKES A ROWDY RUFFIAN TO TAME A PACK OF ROWDY RUFFIANS.
OH, DEAR! FIRST THE AIR CONDITIONING GOES AND NOW THIS. PLEASE EXCUSE ME. ONE OF OUR EXHIBITS REQUIRES MY URGENT ATTENTION.
NO PROBLEM. WE'VE GOT MAPS AND BROCHURES. WE'LL BE FINE... AND QUIET!
WAY TO MAKE MRS. RAMIREZ LOOK BAD, GEORGE! GUESS IT'S JUST ANOTHER DAY WHEN YOU'LL BE CROSSED OFF HER LIST OF FAVORITES.
GEORGE CAN USUALLY IGNORE DIERDRE'S NOT-SO-NICE COMMENTS, BUT SOME-TIMES IT'S IMPOSSIBLE.
OH, NO! I'VE REALLY UPSET MRS. RAMIREZ!
SHE HAS A LIST OF FAVORITES?
OH, FORGET ABOUT IT. LET'S GO GET ENRICHED!

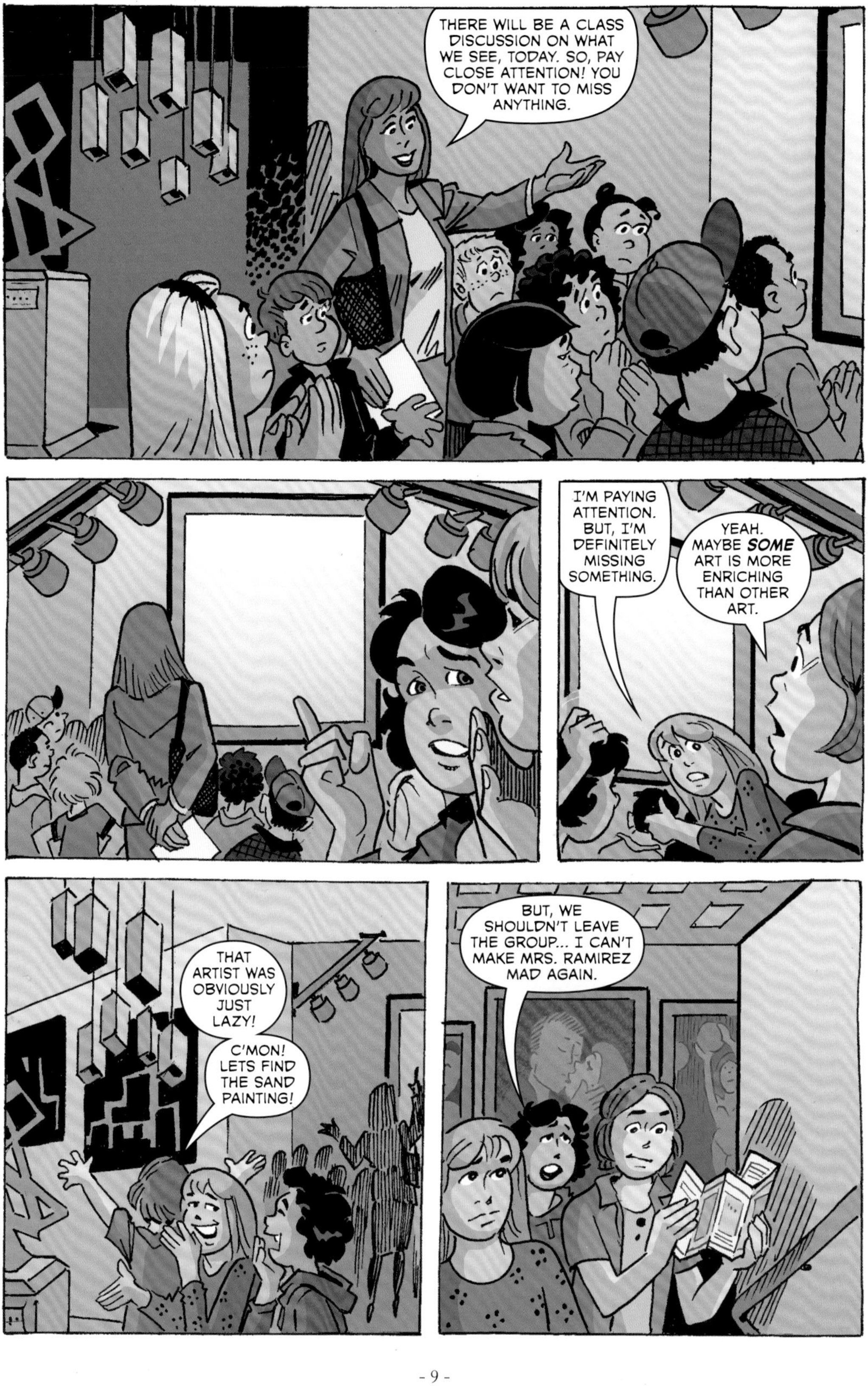
THERE WILL BE A CLASS DISCUSSION ON WHAT WE SEE, TODAY. SO, PAY CLOSE ATTENTION! YOU DON'T WANT TO MISS ANYTHING.
I'M PAYING ATTENTION. BUT, I'M DEFINITELY MISSING SOMETHING.
YEAH. MAYBE **SOME** ART IS MORE ENRICHING THAN OTHER ART.
THAT ARTIST WAS OBVIOUSLY JUST LAZY!
C'MON! LETS FIND THE SAND PAINTING!
BUT, WE SHOULDN'T LEAVE THE GROUP... I CAN'T MAKE MRS. RAMIREZ MAD AGAIN.

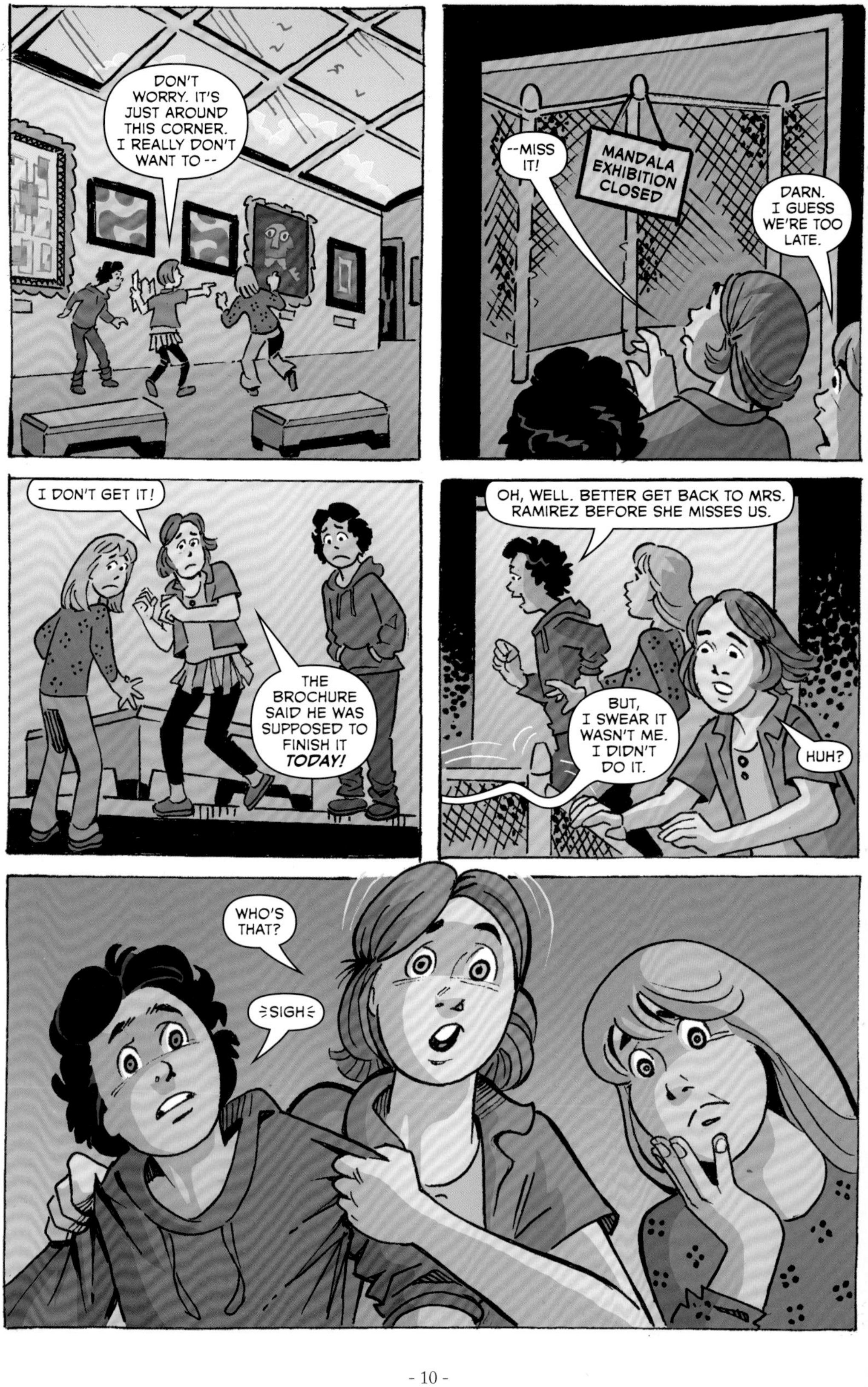
DON'T WORRY. IT'S JUST AROUND THIS CORNER. I REALLY DON'T WANT TO --
--MISS IT!
MANDALA EXHIBITION CLOSED
DARN. I GUESS WE'RE TOO LATE.
I DON'T GET IT!
THE BROCHURE SAID HE WAS SUPPOSED TO FINISH IT *TODAY!*
OH, WELL. BETTER GET BACK TO MRS. RAMIREZ BEFORE SHE MISSES US.
BUT, I SWEAR IT WASN'T ME. I DIDN'T DO IT.
HUH?
WHO'S THAT?
SIGH

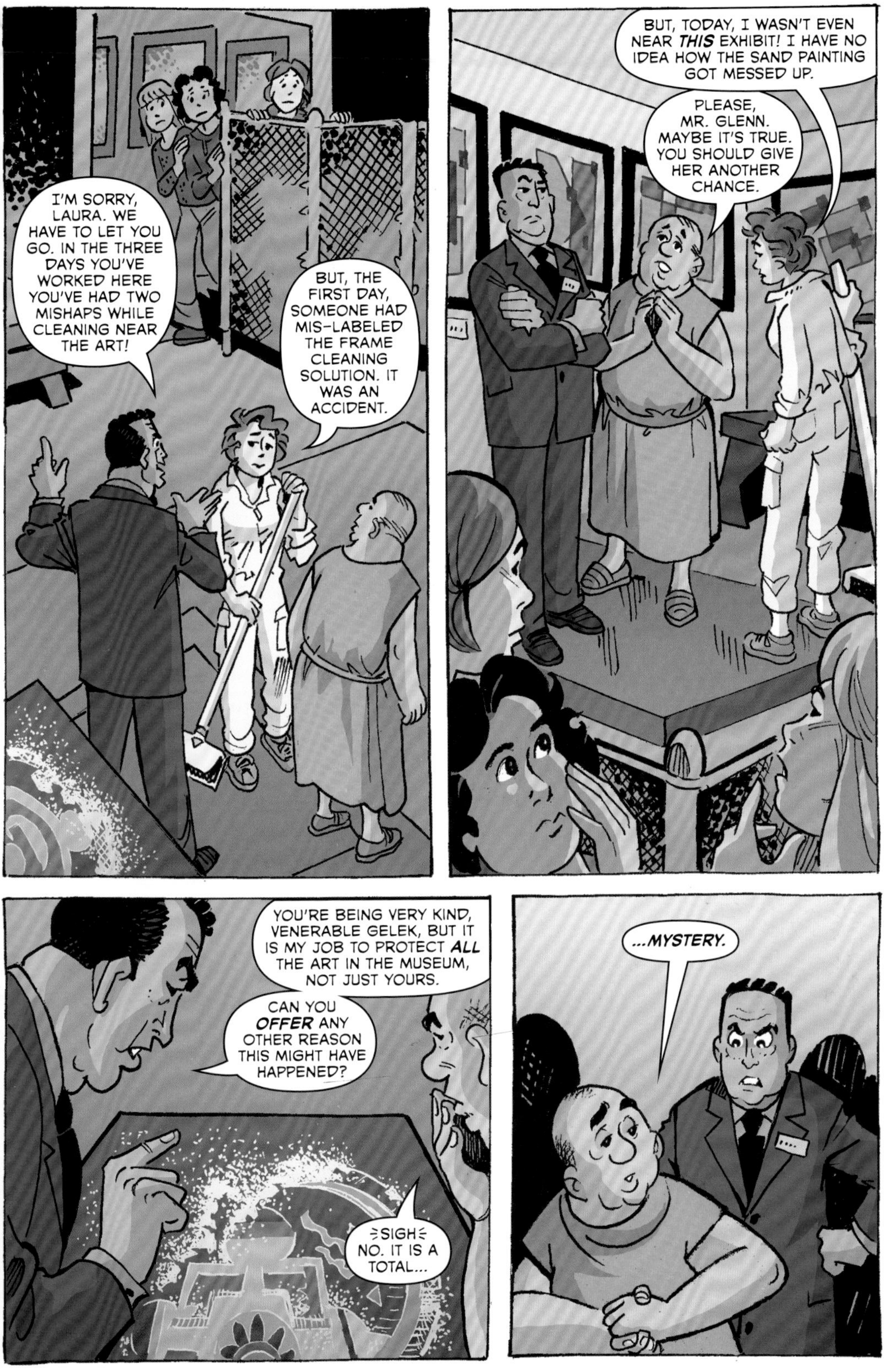
I'M SORRY, LAURA. WE HAVE TO LET YOU GO. IN THE THREE DAYS YOU'VE WORKED HERE YOU'VE HAD TWO MISHAPS WHILE CLEANING NEAR THE ART!
BUT, THE FIRST DAY, SOMEONE HAD MIS-LABELED THE FRAME CLEANING SOLUTION. IT WAS AN ACCIDENT.
BUT, TODAY, I WASN'T EVEN NEAR ***THIS*** EXHIBIT! I HAVE NO IDEA HOW THE SAND PAINTING GOT MESSED UP.
PLEASE, MR. GLENN. MAYBE IT'S TRUE. YOU SHOULD GIVE HER ANOTHER CHANCE.
YOU'RE BEING VERY KIND, VENERABLE GELEK, BUT IT IS MY JOB TO PROTECT ***ALL*** THE ART IN THE MUSEUM, NOT JUST YOURS.
CAN YOU ***OFFER*** ANY OTHER REASON THIS MIGHT HAVE HAPPENED?
⋚SIGH⋚ NO. IT IS A TOTAL...
...MYSTERY.

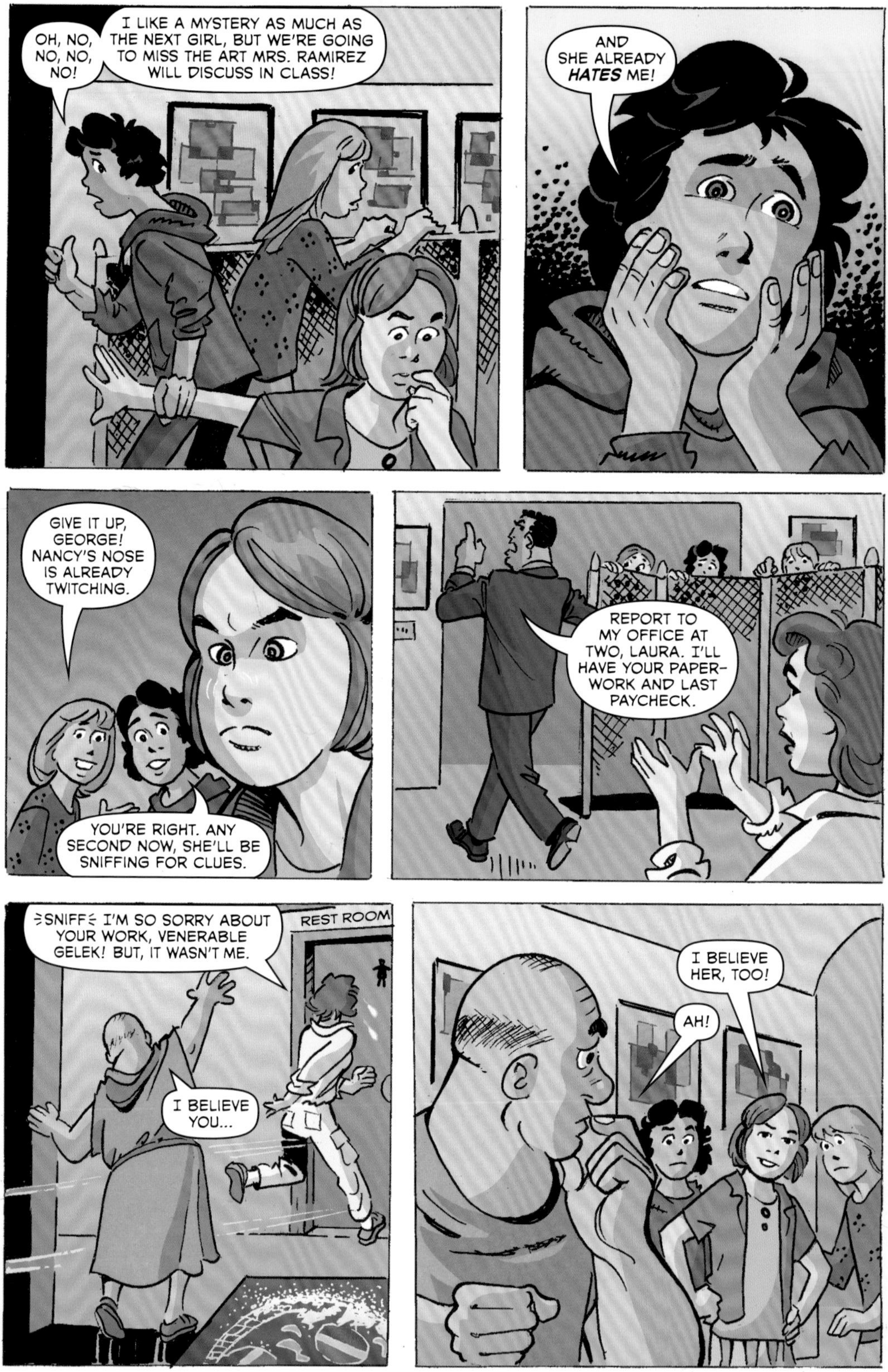
OH, NO, NO, NO, NO!
I LIKE A MYSTERY AS MUCH AS THE NEXT GIRL, BUT WE'RE GOING TO MISS THE ART MRS. RAMIREZ WILL DISCUSS IN CLASS!
AND SHE ALREADY HATES ME!
GIVE IT UP, GEORGE! NANCY'S NOSE IS ALREADY TWITCHING.
YOU'RE RIGHT. ANY SECOND NOW, SHE'LL BE SNIFFING FOR CLUES.
REPORT TO MY OFFICE AT TWO, LAURA. I'LL HAVE YOUR PAPER-WORK AND LAST PAYCHECK.
REST ROOM
SNIFF I'M SO SORRY ABOUT YOUR WORK, VENERABLE GELEK! BUT, IT WASN'T ME.
I BELIEVE YOU...
I BELIEVE HER, TOO!
AH!

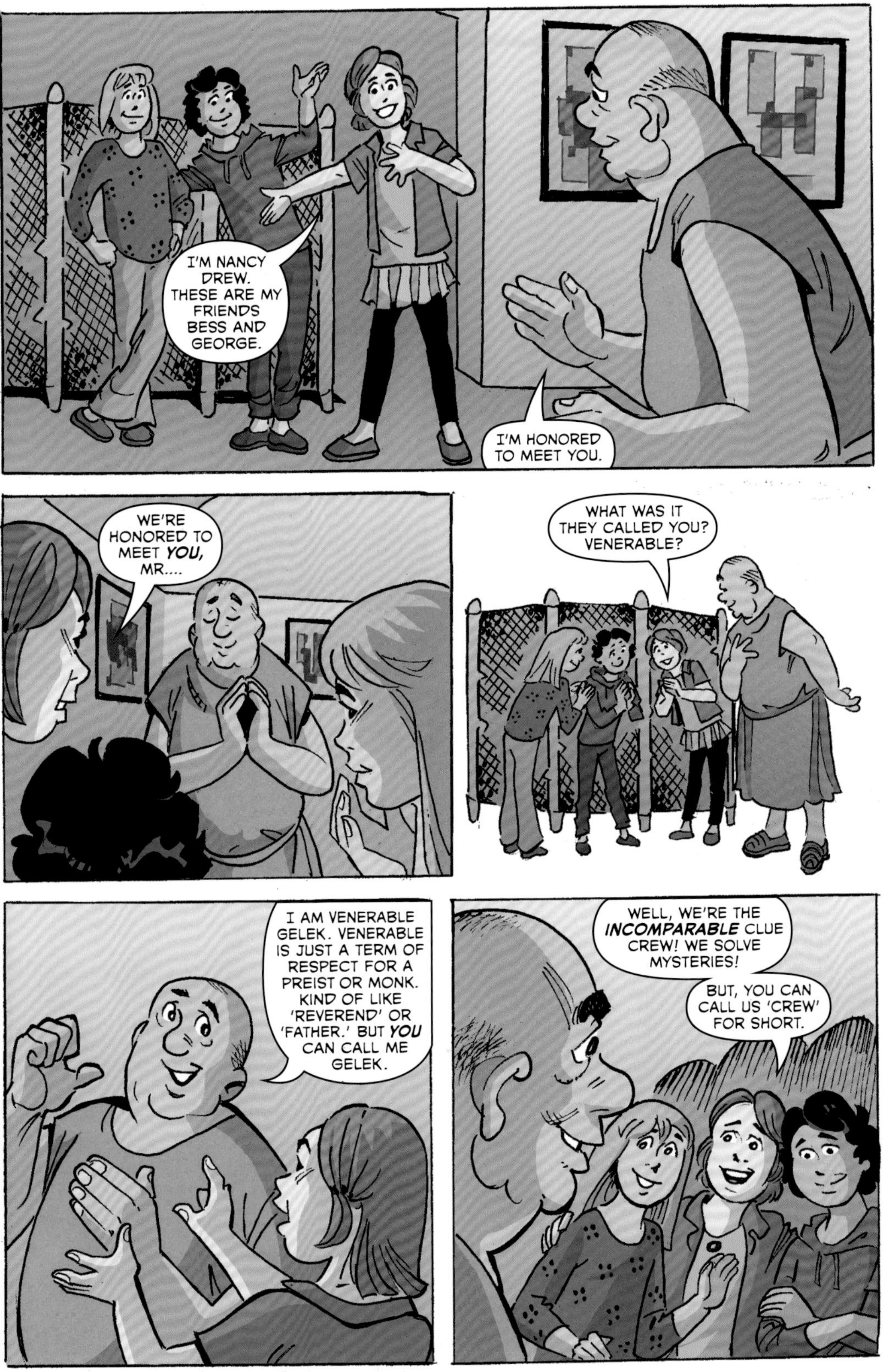
I'M NANCY DREW. THESE ARE MY FRIENDS BESS AND GEORGE.
I'M HONORED TO MEET YOU.
WE'RE HONORED TO MEET *YOU,* MR....
WHAT WAS IT THEY CALLED YOU? VENERABLE?
I AM VENERABLE GELEK. VENERABLE IS JUST A TERM OF RESPECT FOR A PREIST OR MONK. KIND OF LIKE 'REVEREND' OR 'FATHER.' BUT *YOU* CAN CALL ME GELEK.
WELL, WE'RE THE *INCOMPARABLE* CLUE CREW! WE SOLVE MYSTERIES!
BUT, YOU CAN CALL US 'CREW' FOR SHORT.

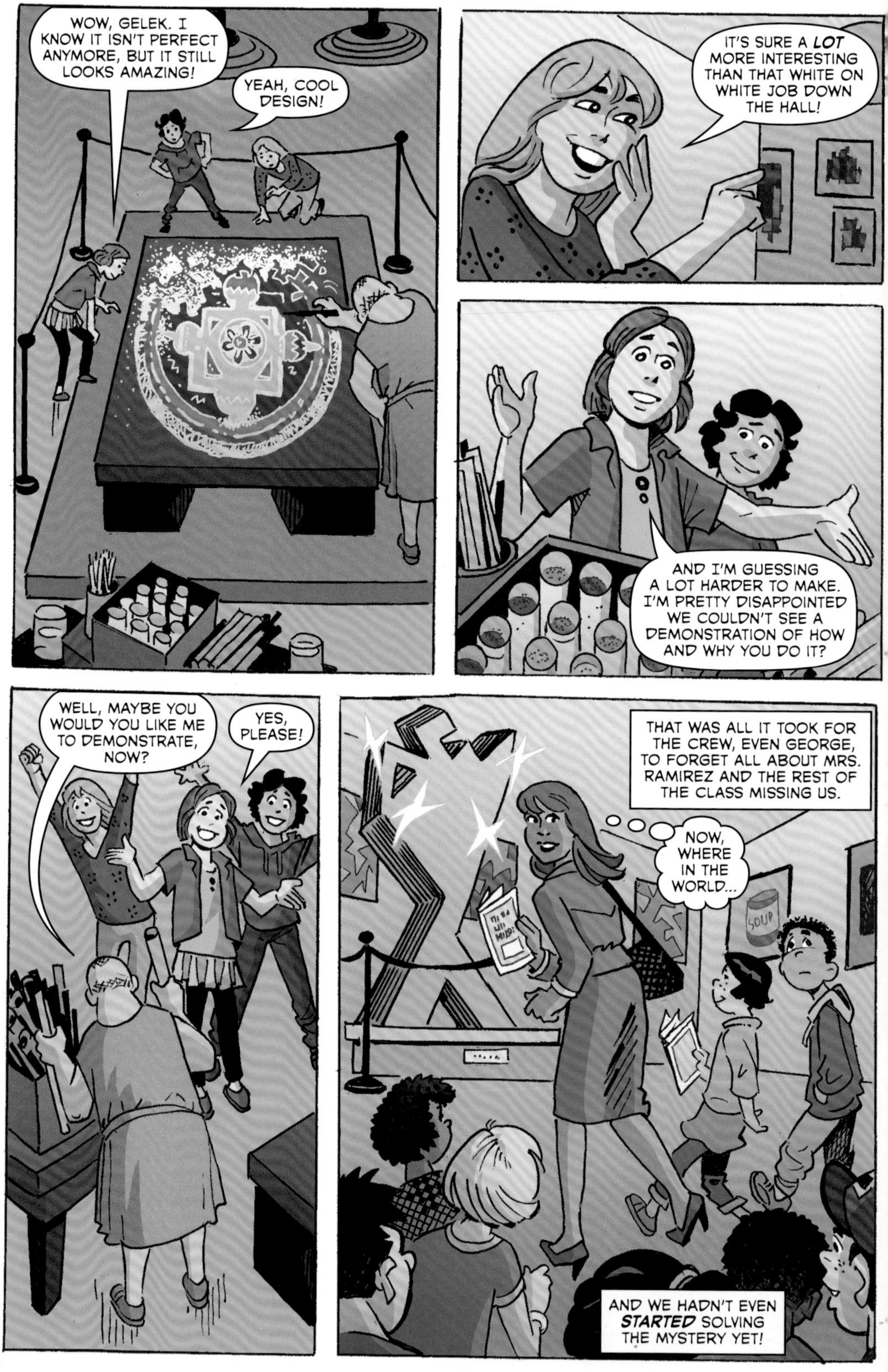
WOW, GELEK. I KNOW IT ISN'T PERFECT ANYMORE, BUT IT STILL LOOKS AMAZING!
YEAH, COOL DESIGN!
IT'S SURE A *LOT* MORE INTERESTING THAN THAT WHITE ON WHITE JOB DOWN THE HALL!
AND I'M GUESSING A LOT HARDER TO MAKE. I'M PRETTY DISAPPOINTED WE COULDN'T SEE A DEMONSTRATION OF HOW AND WHY YOU DO IT?
WELL, MAYBE YOU WOULD YOU LIKE ME TO DEMONSTRATE, NOW?
YES, PLEASE!
THAT WAS ALL IT TOOK FOR THE CREW, EVEN GEORGE, TO FORGET ALL ABOUT MRS. RAMIREZ AND THE REST OF THE CLASS MISSING US.
NOW, WHERE IN THE WORLD...
SOUP
AND WE HADN'T EVEN *STARTED* SOLVING THE MYSTERY YET!

CHAPTER 2: BEAUTY AND THE PRIEST

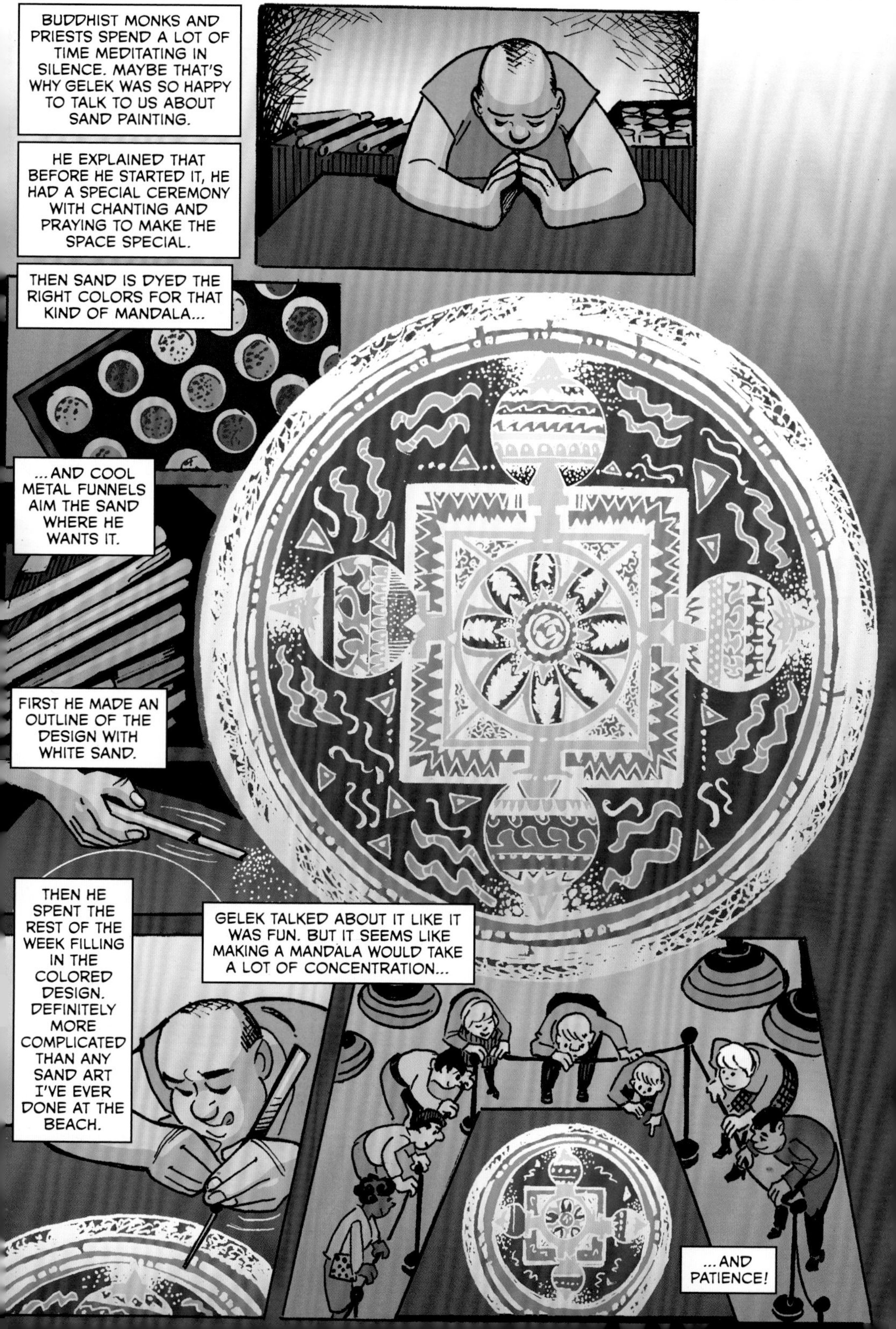
BUDDHIST MONKS AND PRIESTS SPEND A LOT OF TIME MEDITATING IN SILENCE. MAYBE THAT'S WHY GELEK WAS SO HAPPY TO TALK TO US ABOUT SAND PAINTING.
HE EXPLAINED THAT BEFORE HE STARTED IT, HE HAD A SPECIAL CEREMONY WITH CHANTING AND PRAYING TO MAKE THE SPACE SPECIAL.
THEN SAND IS DYED THE RIGHT COLORS FOR THAT KIND OF MANDALA...
...AND COOL METAL FUNNELS AIM THE SAND WHERE HE WANTS IT.
FIRST HE MADE AN OUTLINE OF THE DESIGN WITH WHITE SAND.
THEN HE SPENT THE REST OF THE WEEK FILLING IN THE COLORED DESIGN. DEFINITELY MORE COMPLICATED THAN ANY SAND ART I'VE EVER DONE AT THE BEACH.
GELEK TALKED ABOUT IT LIKE IT WAS FUN. BUT IT SEEMS LIKE MAKING A MANDALA WOULD TAKE A LOT OF CONCENTRATION...
...AND PATIENCE!

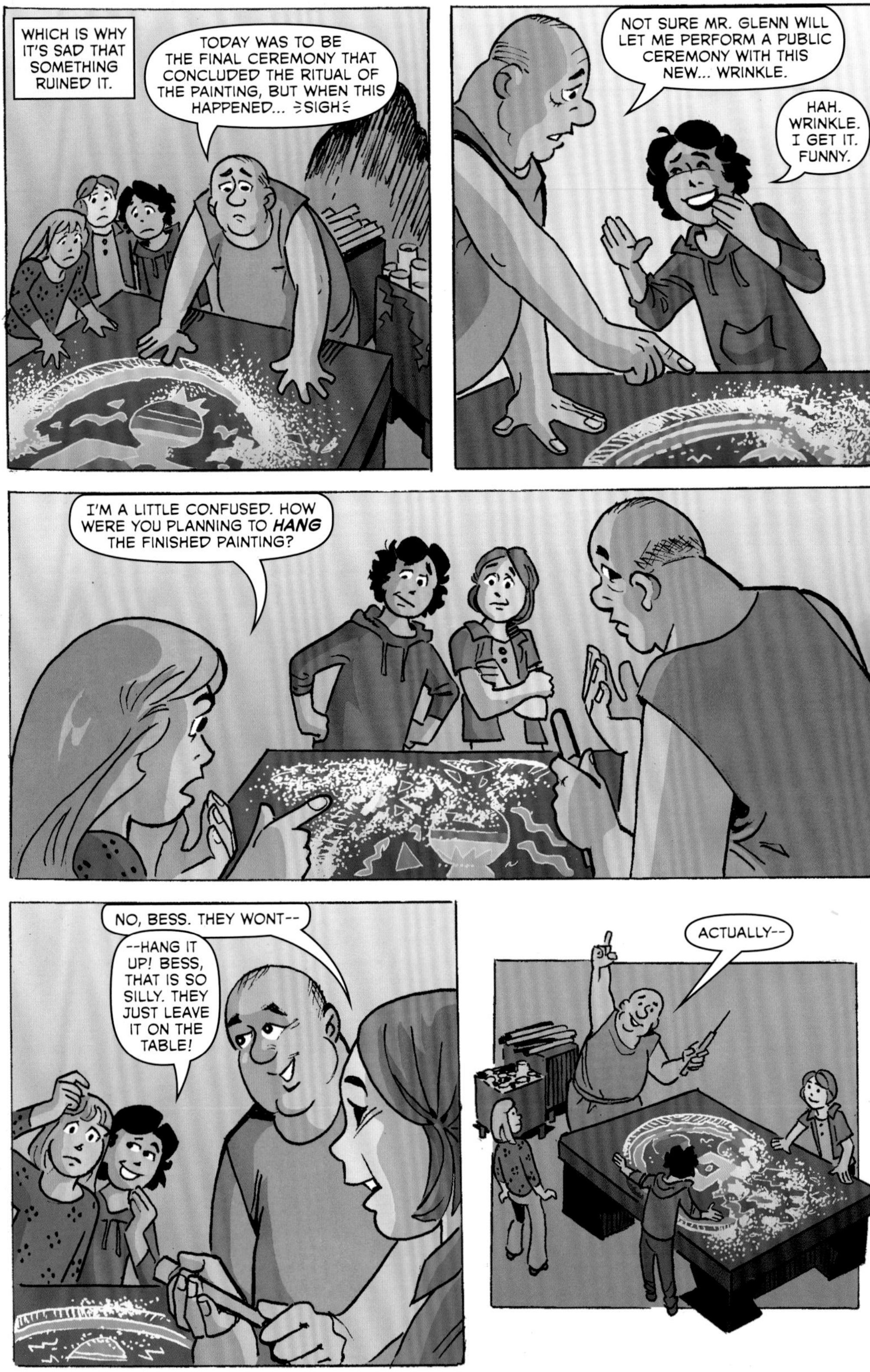
WHICH IS WHY IT'S SAD THAT SOMETHING RUINED IT.
TODAY WAS TO BE THE FINAL CEREMONY THAT CONCLUDED THE RITUAL OF THE PAINTING, BUT WHEN THIS HAPPENED... SIGH
NOT SURE MR. GLENN WILL LET ME PERFORM A PUBLIC CEREMONY WITH THIS NEW... WRINKLE.
HAH. WRINKLE. I GET IT. FUNNY.
I'M A LITTLE CONFUSED. HOW WERE YOU PLANNING TO HANG THE FINISHED PAINTING?
NO, BESS. THEY WONT--
--HANG IT UP! BESS, THAT IS SO SILLY. THEY JUST LEAVE IT ON THE TABLE!
ACTUALLY--

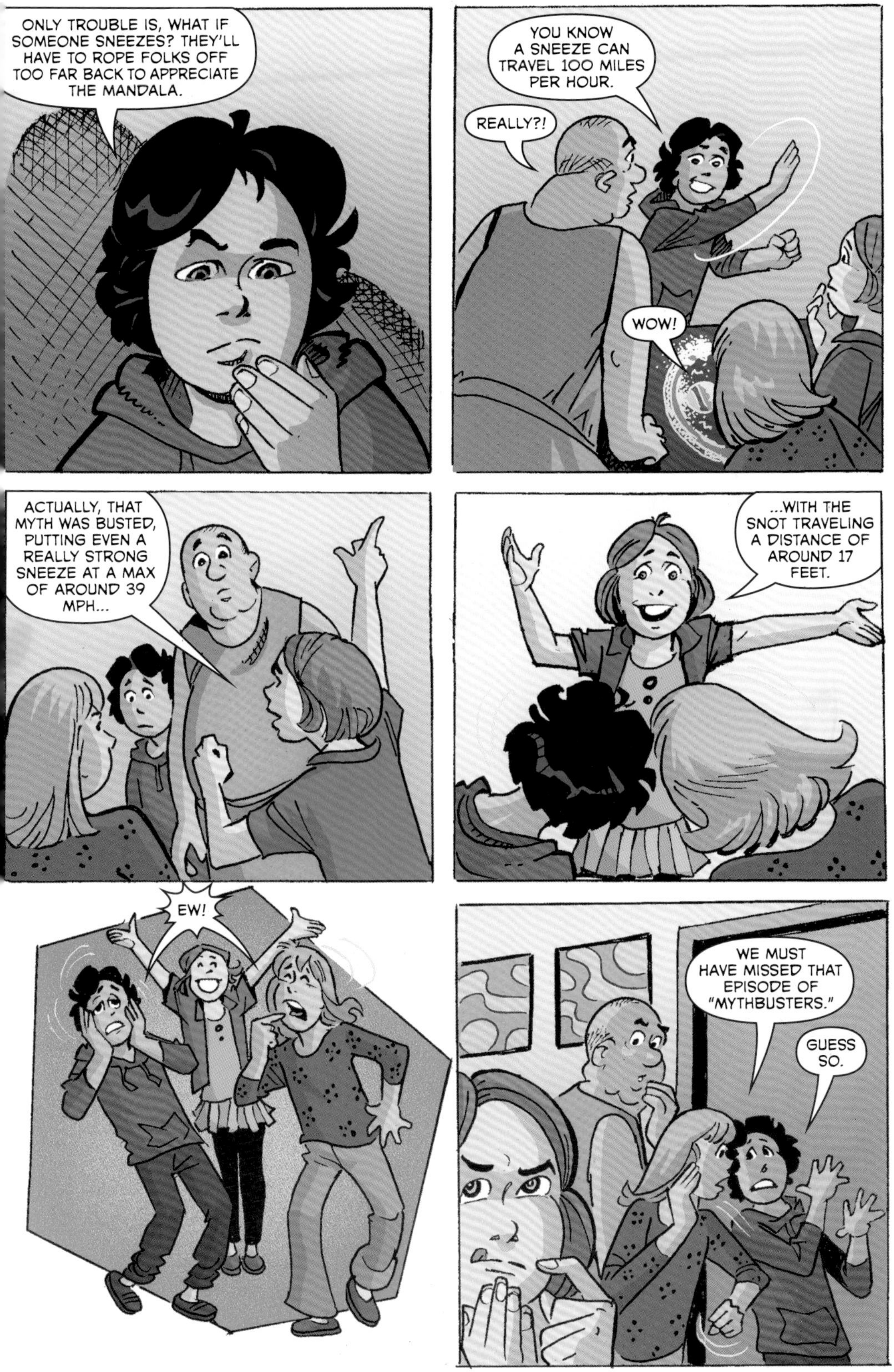
ONLY TROUBLE IS, WHAT IF SOMEONE SNEEZES? THEY'LL HAVE TO ROPE FOLKS OFF TOO FAR BACK TO APPRECIATE THE MANDALA.
YOU KNOW A SNEEZE CAN TRAVEL 100 MILES PER HOUR.
REALLY?!
WOW!
ACTUALLY, THAT MYTH WAS BUSTED, PUTTING EVEN A REALLY STRONG SNEEZE AT A MAX OF AROUND 39 MPH...
...WITH THE SNOT TRAVELING A DISTANCE OF AROUND 17 FEET.
EW!
WE MUST HAVE MISSED THAT EPISODE OF "MYTHBUSTERS."
GUESS SO.

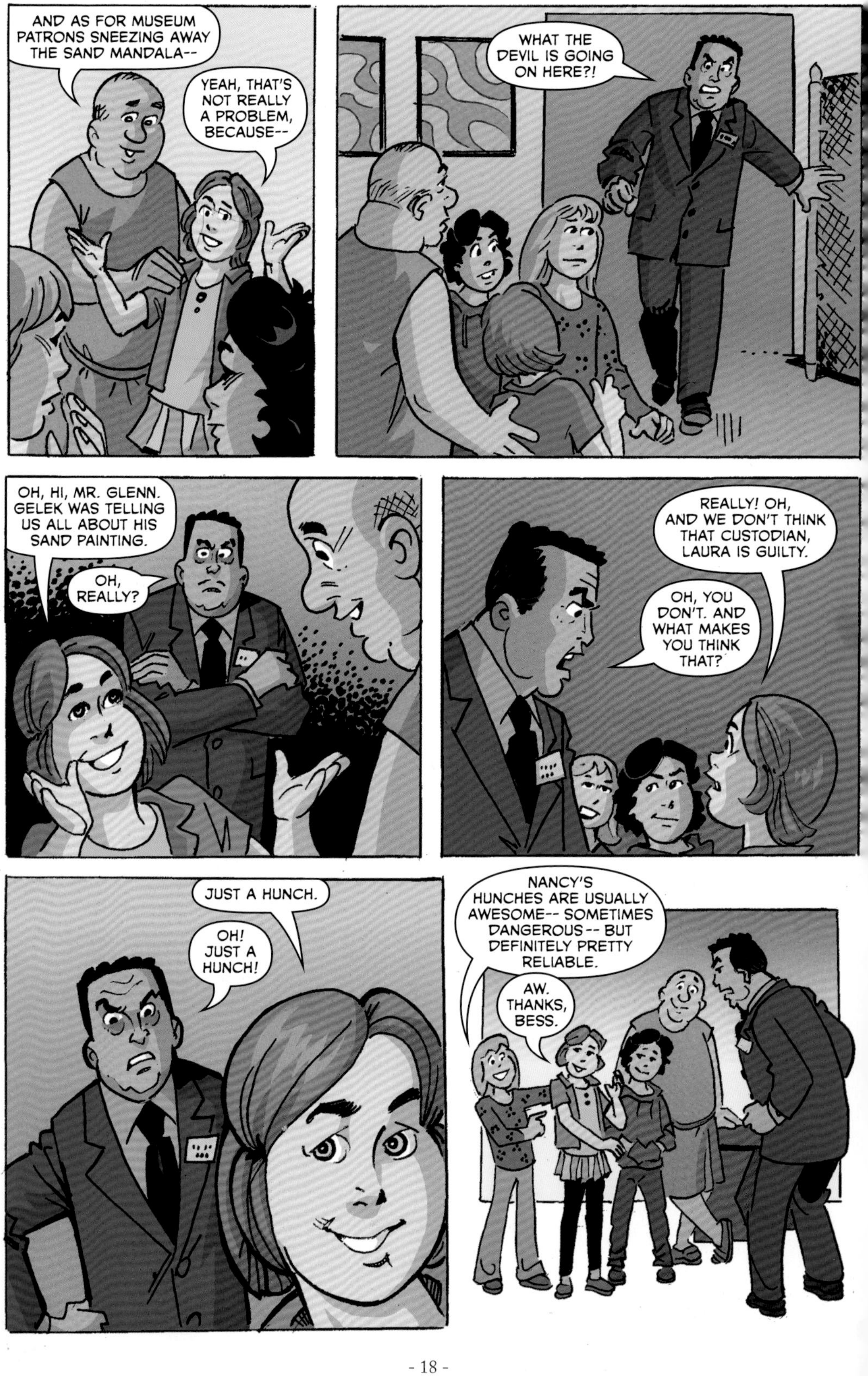
AND AS FOR MUSEUM PATRONS SNEEZING AWAY THE SAND MANDALA--
YEAH, THAT'S NOT REALLY A PROBLEM, BECAUSE--
WHAT THE DEVIL IS GOING ON HERE?!
OH, HI, MR. GLENN. GELEK WAS TELLING US ALL ABOUT HIS SAND PAINTING.
OH, REALLY?
REALLY! OH, AND WE DON'T THINK THAT CUSTODIAN, LAURA IS GUILTY.
OH, YOU DON'T. AND WHAT MAKES YOU THINK THAT?
JUST A HUNCH.
OH! JUST A HUNCH!
NANCY'S HUNCHES ARE USUALLY AWESOME-- SOMETIMES DANGEROUS-- BUT DEFINITELY PRETTY RELIABLE.
AW. THANKS, BESS.

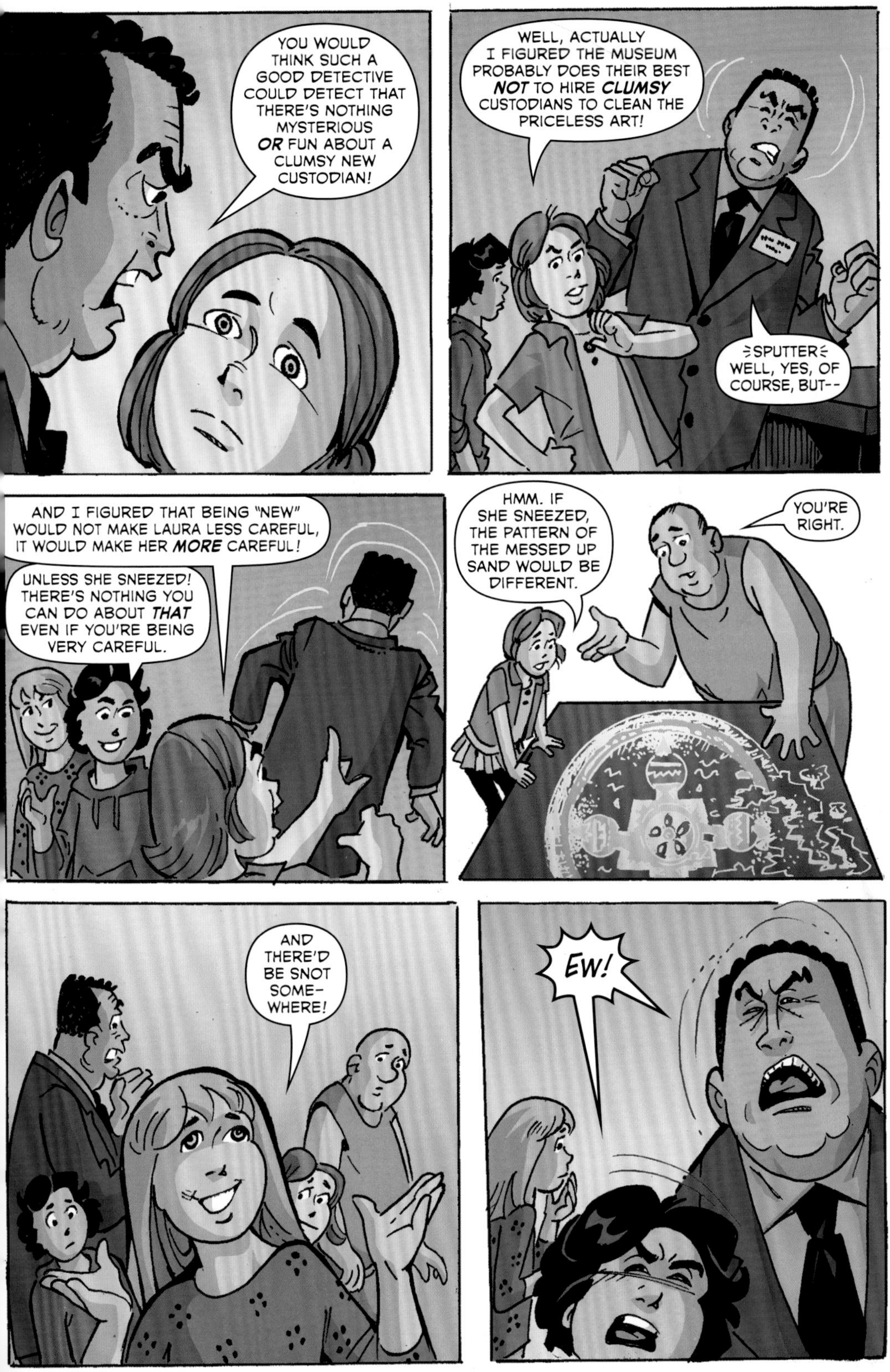
YOU WOULD THINK SUCH A GOOD DETECTIVE COULD DETECT THAT THERE'S NOTHING MYSTERIOUS *OR* FUN ABOUT A CLUMSY NEW CUSTODIAN!
WELL, ACTUALLY I FIGURED THE MUSEUM PROBABLY DOES THEIR BEST *NOT* TO HIRE *CLUMSY* CUSTODIANS TO CLEAN THE PRICELESS ART!
⋞SPUTTER⋟ WELL, YES, OF COURSE, BUT--
AND I FIGURED THAT BEING "NEW" WOULD NOT MAKE LAURA LESS CAREFUL, IT WOULD MAKE HER *MORE* CAREFUL!
UNLESS SHE SNEEZED! THERE'S NOTHING YOU CAN DO ABOUT *THAT* EVEN IF YOU'RE BEING VERY CAREFUL.
HMM. IF SHE SNEEZED, THE PATTERN OF THE MESSED UP SAND WOULD BE DIFFERENT.
YOU'RE RIGHT.
AND THERE'D BE SNOT SOME-WHERE!
EW!

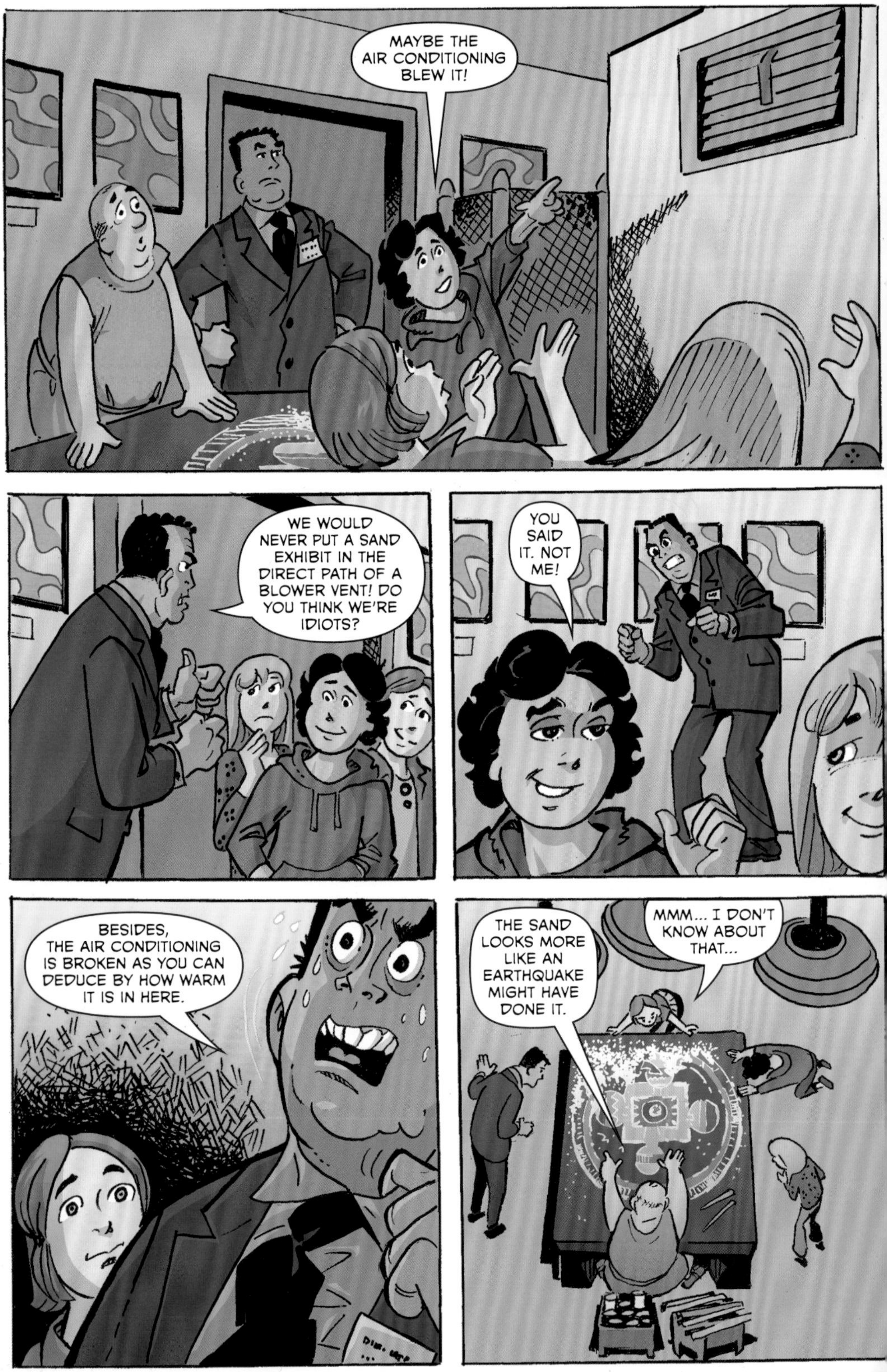
MAYBE THE AIR CONDITIONING BLEW IT!
WE WOULD NEVER PUT A SAND EXHIBIT IN THE DIRECT PATH OF A BLOWER VENT! DO YOU THINK WE'RE IDIOTS?
YOU SAID IT. NOT ME!
BESIDES, THE AIR CONDITIONING IS BROKEN AS YOU CAN DEDUCE BY HOW WARM IT IS IN HERE.
THE SAND LOOKS MORE LIKE AN EARTHQUAKE MIGHT HAVE DONE IT.
MMM... I DON'T KNOW ABOUT THAT...

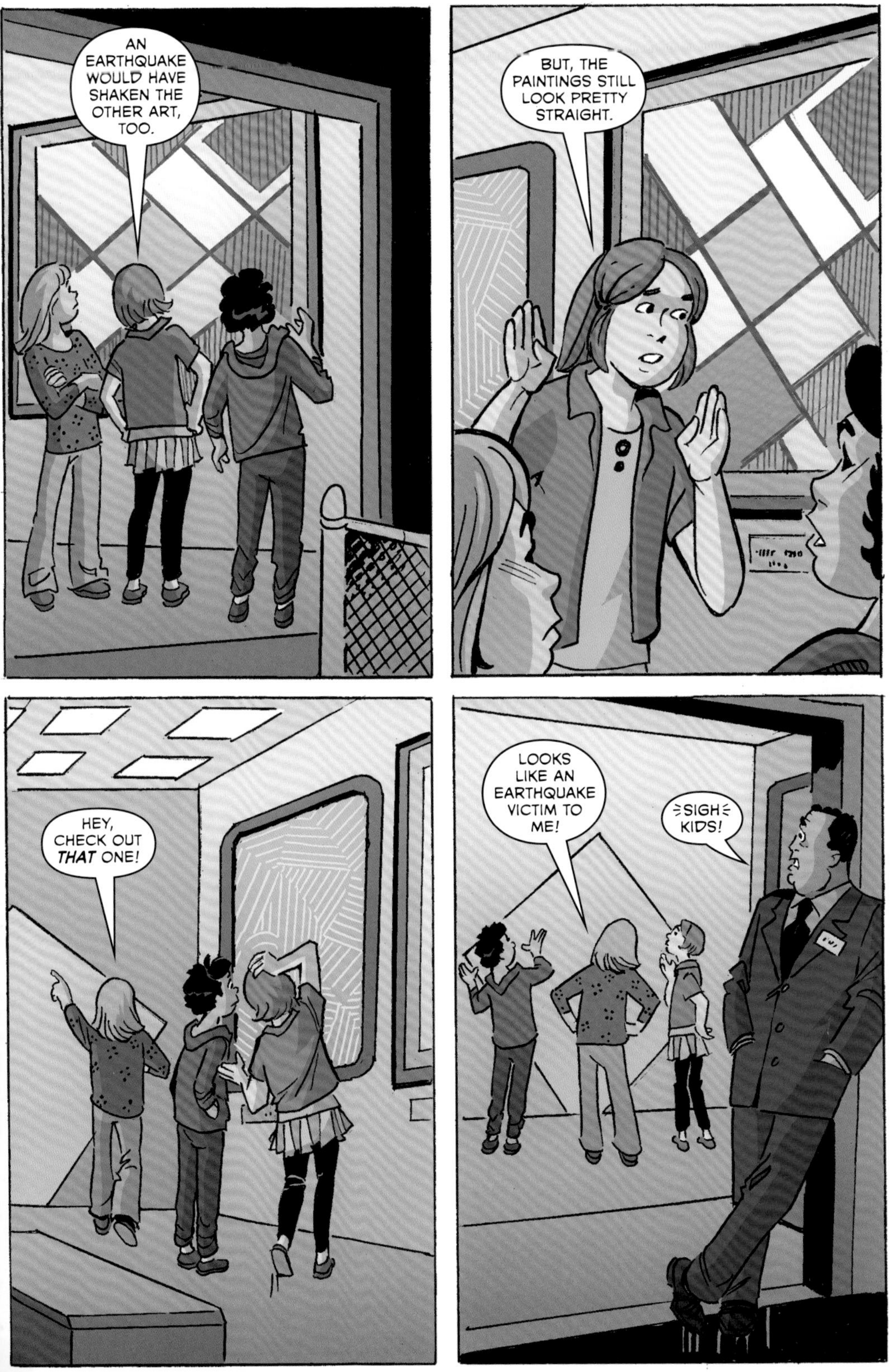
AN EARTHQUAKE WOULD HAVE SHAKEN THE OTHER ART, TOO.
BUT, THE PAINTINGS STILL LOOK PRETTY STRAIGHT.
HEY, CHECK OUT *THAT* ONE!
LOOKS LIKE AN EARTHQUAKE VICTIM TO ME!
SIGH KIDS!

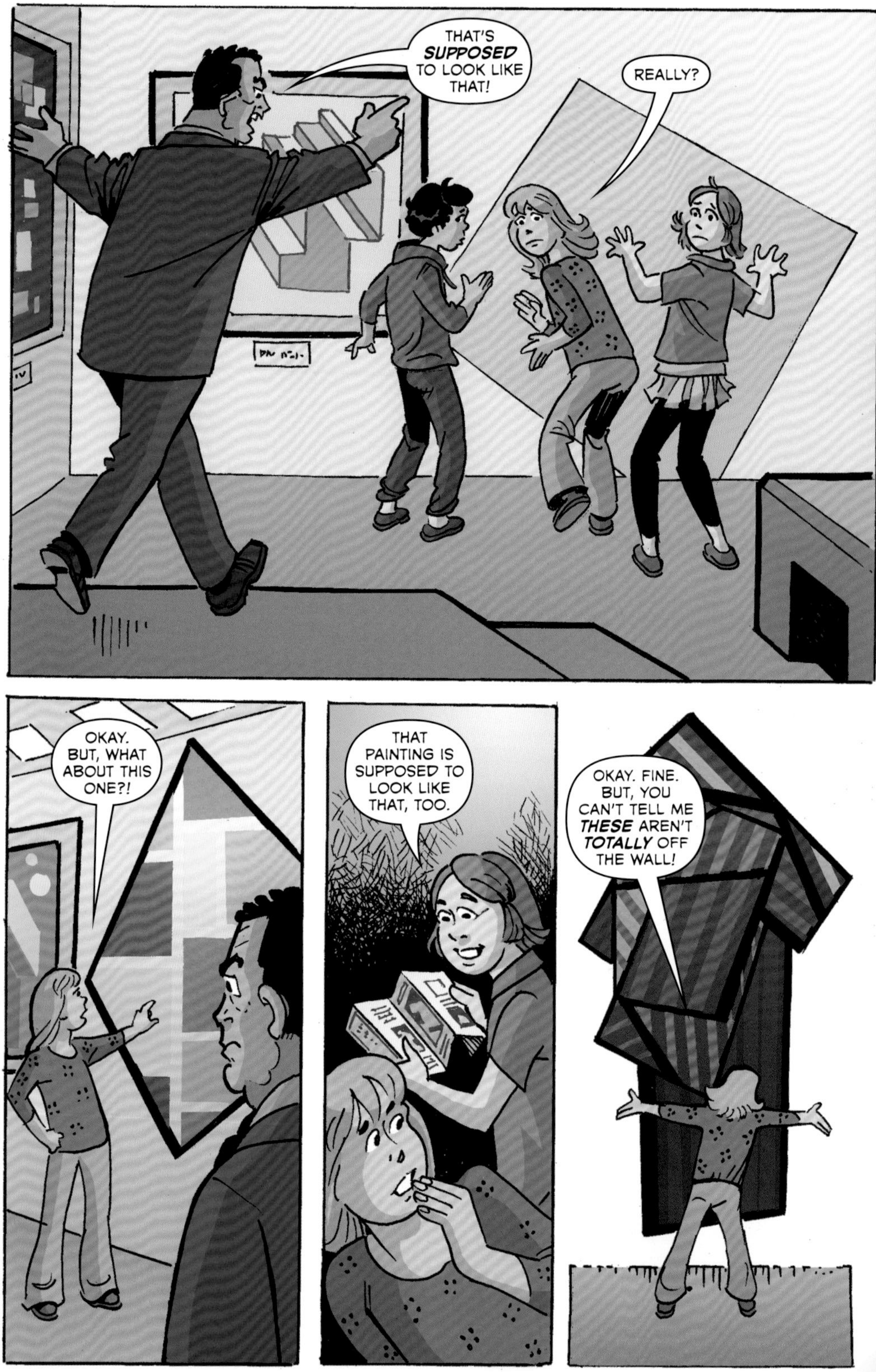
THAT'S SUPPOSED TO LOOK LIKE THAT!
REALLY?
OKAY. BUT, WHAT ABOUT THIS ONE?!
THAT PAINTING IS SUPPOSED TO LOOK LIKE THAT, TOO.
OKAY. FINE. BUT, YOU CAN'T TELL ME THESE AREN'T TOTALLY OFF THE WALL!

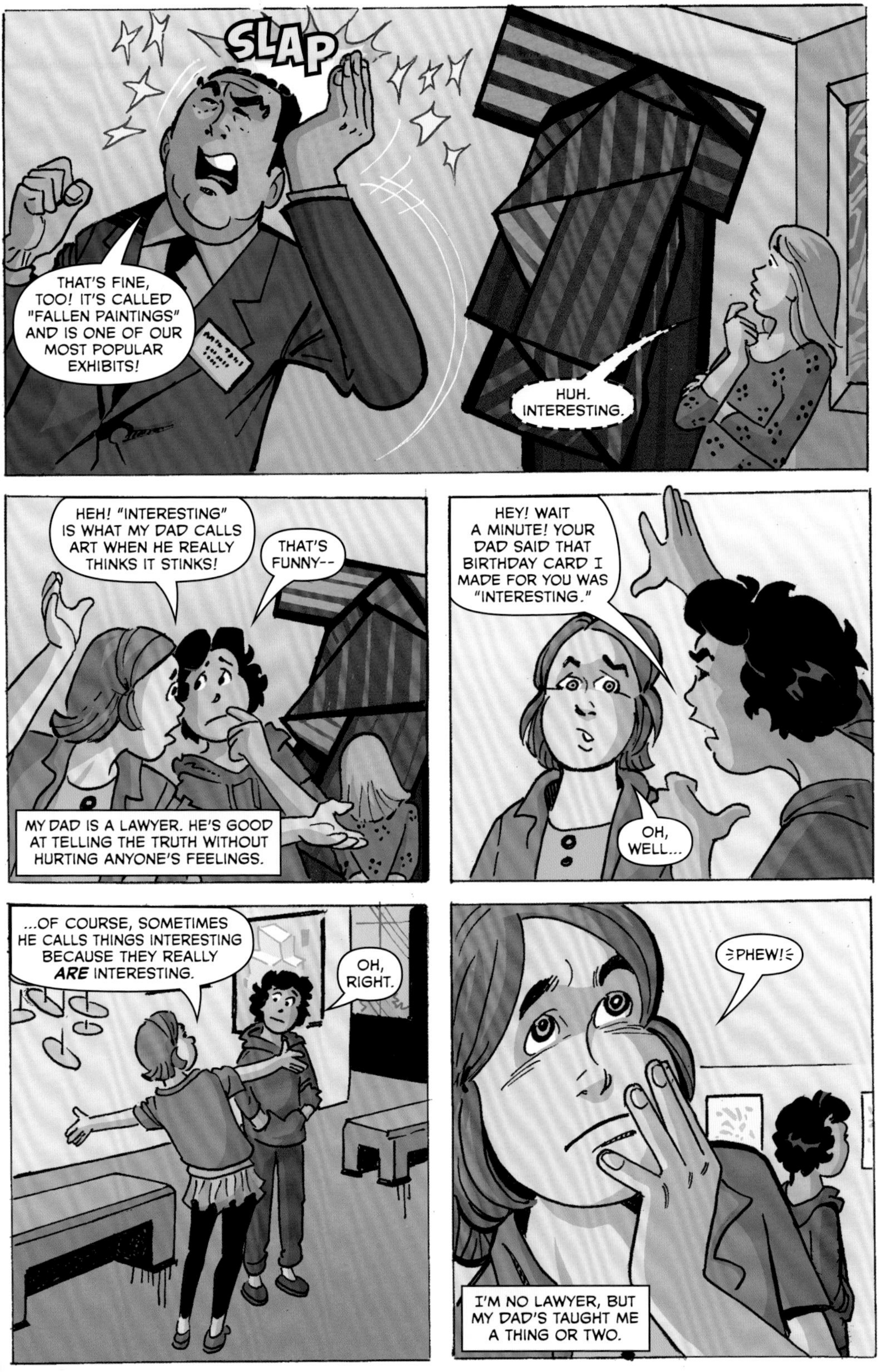
SLAP
THAT'S FINE, TOO! IT'S CALLED "FALLEN PAINTINGS" AND IS ONE OF OUR MOST POPULAR EXHIBITS!
HUH. INTERESTING.
HEH! "INTERESTING" IS WHAT MY DAD CALLS ART WHEN HE REALLY THINKS IT STINKS!
THAT'S FUNNY--
MY DAD IS A LAWYER. HE'S GOOD AT TELLING THE TRUTH WITHOUT HURTING ANYONE'S FEELINGS.
HEY! WAIT A MINUTE! YOUR DAD SAID THAT BIRTHDAY CARD I MADE FOR YOU WAS "INTERESTING."
OH, WELL...
...OF COURSE, SOMETIMES HE CALLS THINGS INTERESTING BECAUSE THEY REALLY ARE INTERESTING.
OH, RIGHT.
PHEW!
I'M NO LAWYER, BUT MY DAD'S TAUGHT ME A THING OR TWO.

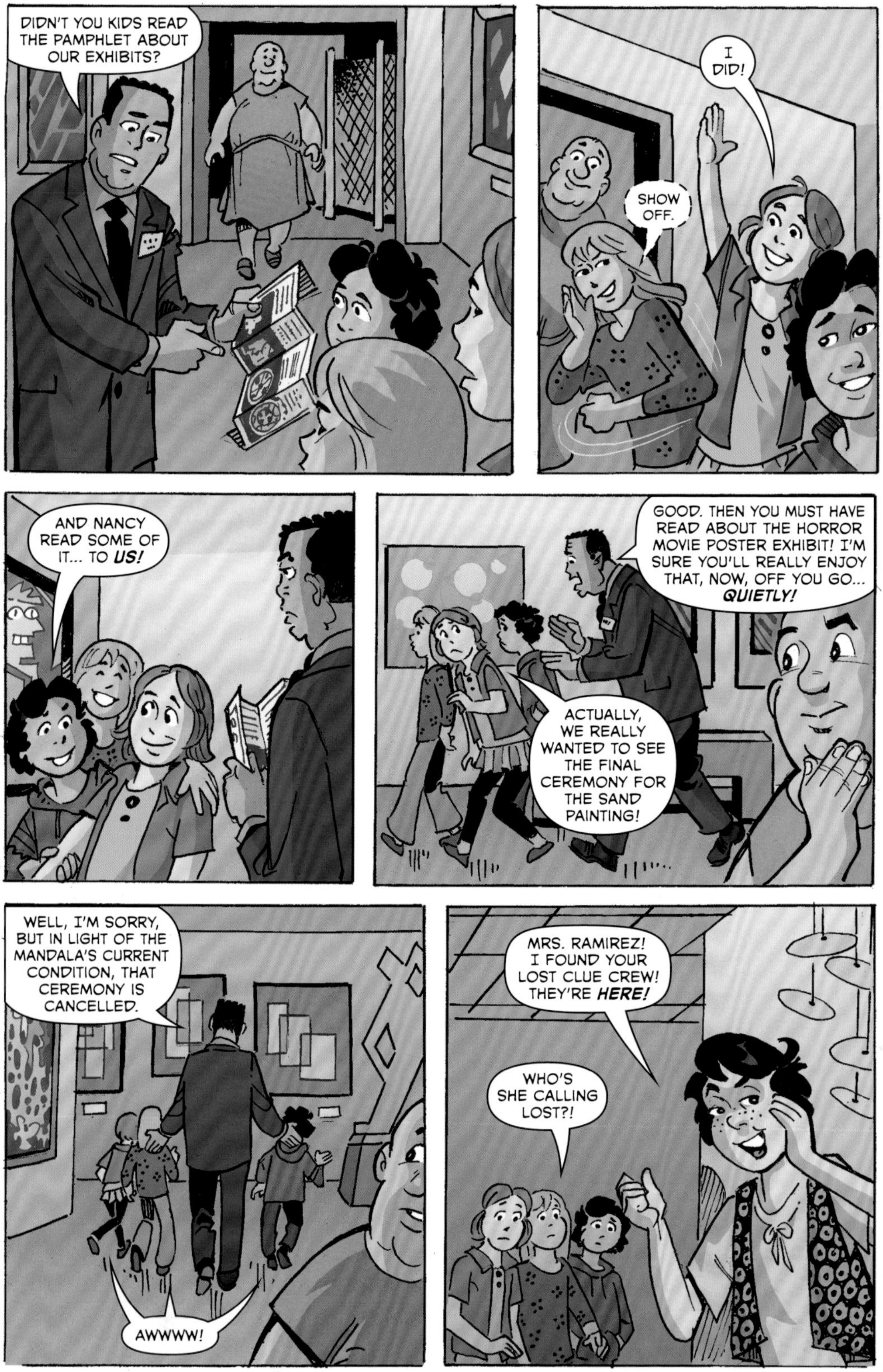
DIDN'T YOU KIDS READ THE PAMPHLET ABOUT OUR EXHIBITS?
I DID!
SHOW OFF.
AND NANCY READ SOME OF IT... TO US!
GOOD. THEN YOU MUST HAVE READ ABOUT THE HORROR MOVIE POSTER EXHIBIT! I'M SURE YOU'LL REALLY ENJOY THAT, NOW, OFF YOU GO... QUIETLY!
ACTUALLY, WE REALLY WANTED TO SEE THE FINAL CEREMONY FOR THE SAND PAINTING!
WELL, I'M SORRY, BUT IN LIGHT OF THE MANDALA'S CURRENT CONDITION, THAT CEREMONY IS CANCELLED.
AWWWW!
MRS. RAMIREZ! I FOUND YOUR LOST CLUE CREW! THEY'RE HERE!
WHO'S SHE CALLING LOST?!

CHAPTER 3: LUNCH AND SYMPATHY

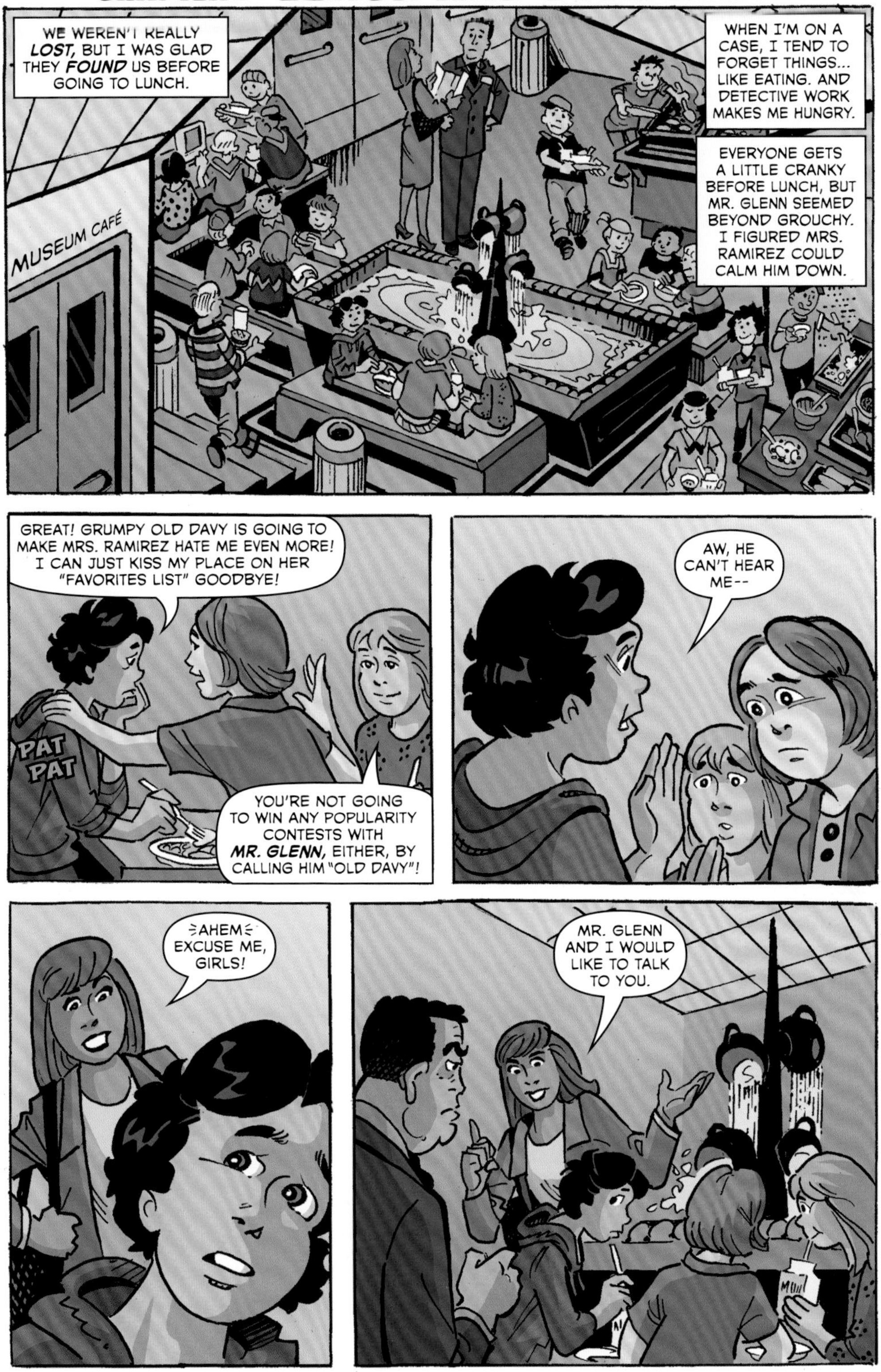

WE WEREN'T REALLY LOST, BUT I WAS GLAD THEY FOUND US BEFORE GOING TO LUNCH.
MUSEUM CAFÉ
WHEN I'M ON A CASE, I TEND TO FORGET THINGS... LIKE EATING. AND DETECTIVE WORK MAKES ME HUNGRY.
EVERYONE GETS A LITTLE CRANKY BEFORE LUNCH, BUT MR. GLENN SEEMED BEYOND GROUCHY. I FIGURED MRS. RAMIREZ COULD CALM HIM DOWN.
GREAT! GRUMPY OLD DAVY IS GOING TO MAKE MRS. RAMIREZ HATE ME EVEN MORE! I CAN JUST KISS MY PLACE ON HER "FAVORITES LIST" GOODBYE!
PAT PAT
YOU'RE NOT GOING TO WIN ANY POPULARITY CONTESTS WITH MR. GLENN, EITHER, BY CALLING HIM "OLD DAVY"!
AW, HE CAN'T HEAR ME--
AHEM EXCUSE ME, GIRLS!
MR. GLENN AND I WOULD LIKE TO TALK TO YOU.

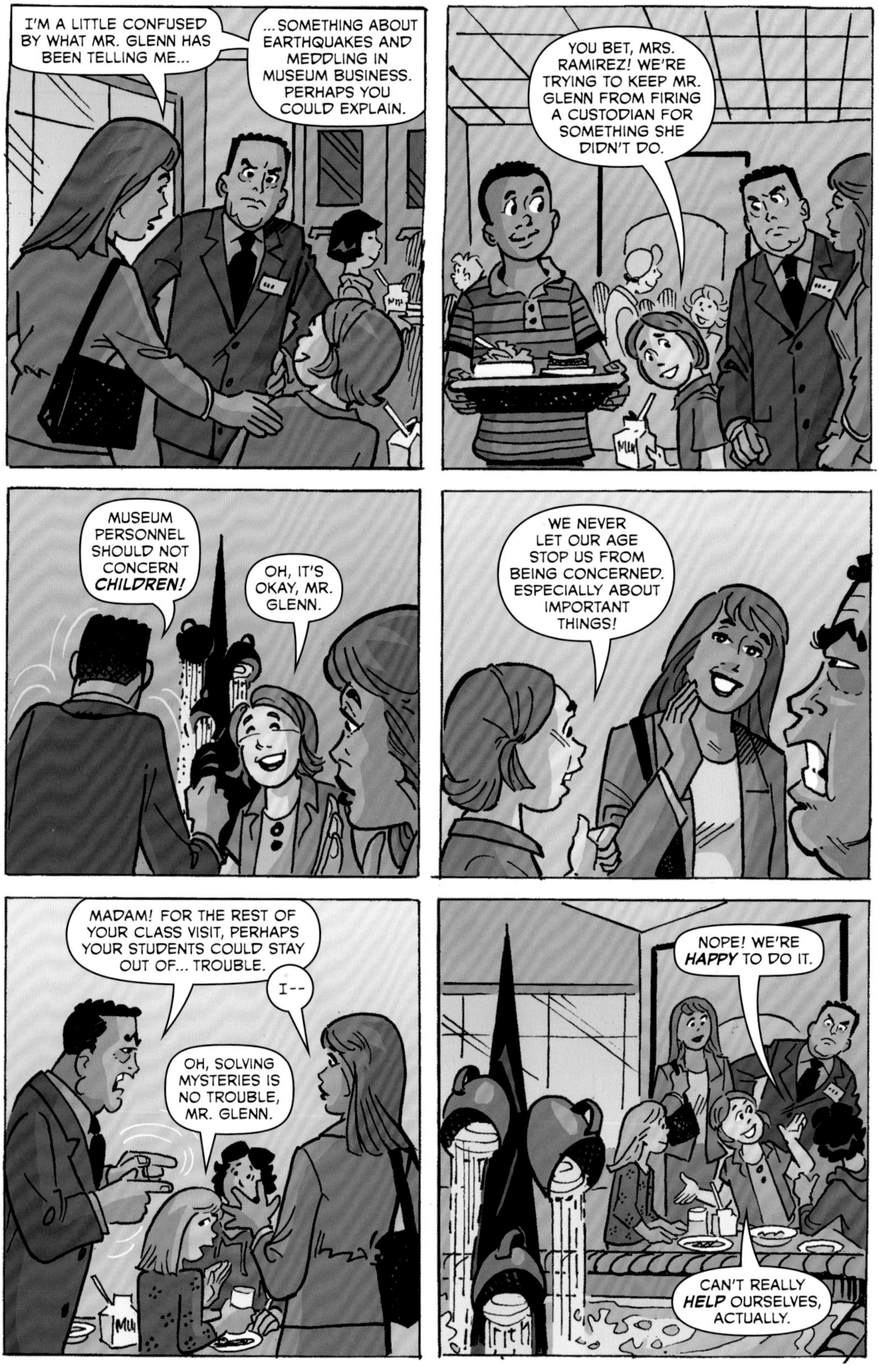
I'M A LITTLE CONFUSED BY WHAT MR. GLENN HAS BEEN TELLING ME...
...SOMETHING ABOUT EARTHQUAKES AND MEDDLING IN MUSEUM BUSINESS. PERHAPS YOU COULD EXPLAIN.
YOU BET, MRS. RAMIREZ! WE'RE TRYING TO KEEP MR. GLENN FROM FIRING A CUSTODIAN FOR SOMETHING SHE DIDN'T DO.
MUSEUM PERSONNEL SHOULD NOT CONCERN *CHILDREN!*
OH, IT'S OKAY, MR. GLENN.
WE NEVER LET OUR AGE STOP US FROM BEING CONCERNED. ESPECIALLY ABOUT IMPORTANT THINGS!
MADAM! FOR THE REST OF YOUR CLASS VISIT, PERHAPS YOUR STUDENTS COULD STAY OUT OF... TROUBLE.
I--
OH, SOLVING MYSTERIES IS NO TROUBLE, MR. GLENN.
NOPE! WE'RE *HAPPY* TO DO IT.
CAN'T REALLY *HELP* OURSELVES, ACTUALLY.

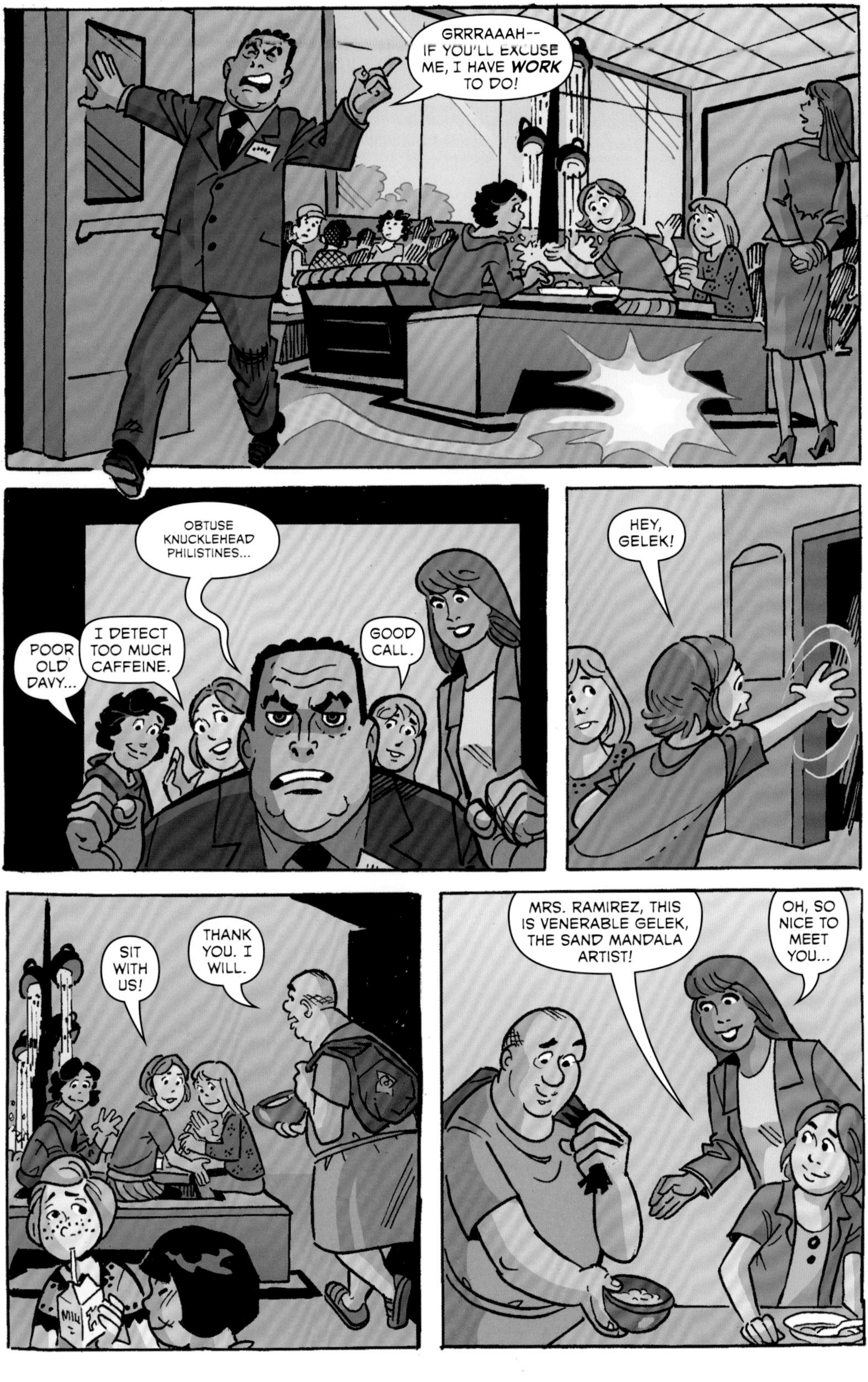
GRRRAAAH-- IF YOU'LL EXCUSE ME, I HAVE *WORK* TO DO!
OBTUSE KNUCKLEHEAD PHILISTINES...
POOR OLD DAVY...
I DETECT TOO MUCH CAFFEINE.
GOOD CALL.
HEY, GELEK!
SIT WITH US!
THANK YOU. I WILL.
MRS. RAMIREZ, THIS IS VENERABLE GELEK, THE SAND MANDALA ARTIST!
OH, SO NICE TO MEET YOU...

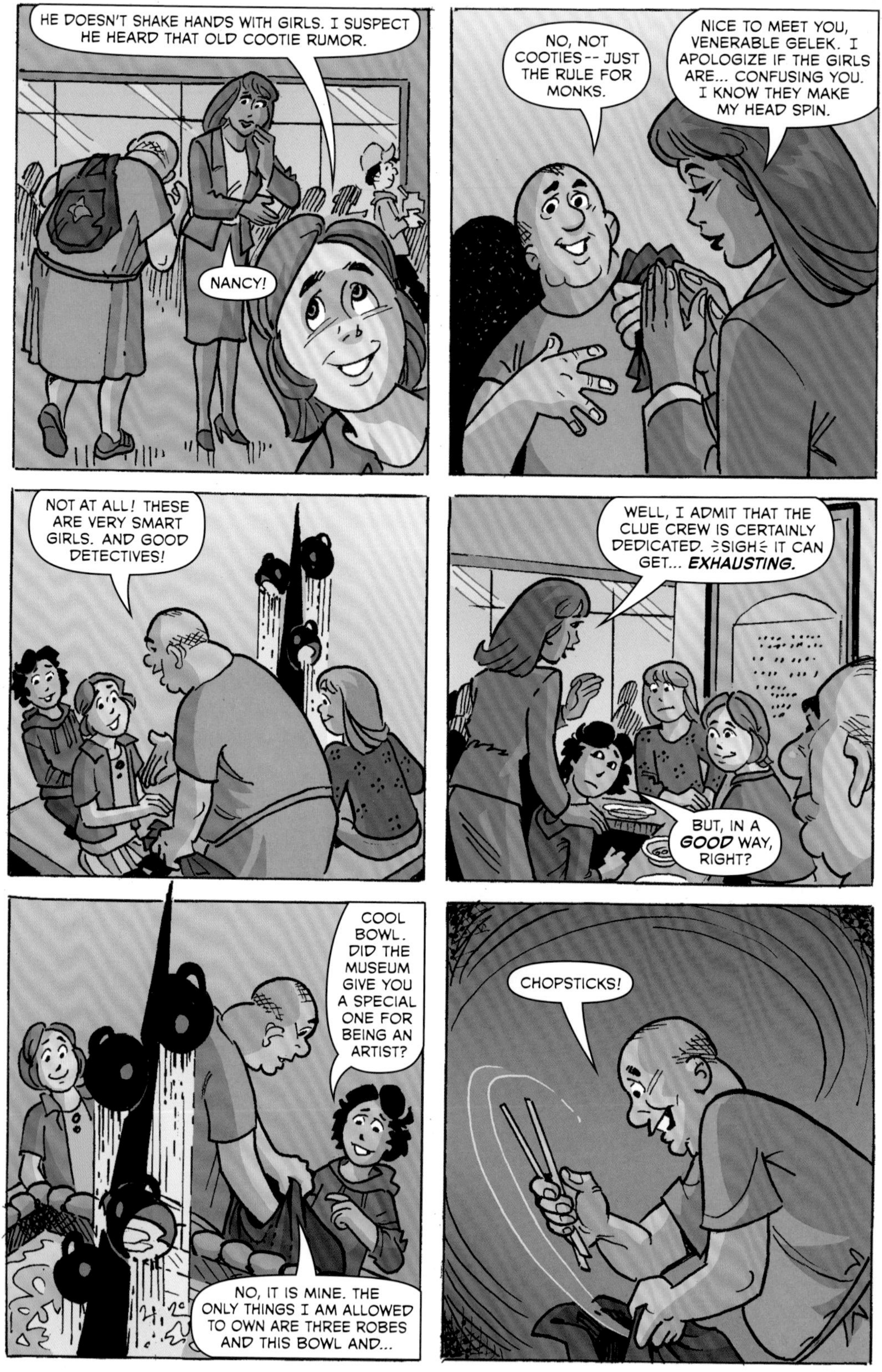

HE DOESN'T SHAKE HANDS WITH GIRLS. I SUSPECT HE HEARD THAT OLD COOTIE RUMOR.
NANCY!
NO, NOT COOTIES -- JUST THE RULE FOR MONKS.
NICE TO MEET YOU, VENERABLE GELEK. I APOLOGIZE IF THE GIRLS ARE... CONFUSING YOU. I KNOW THEY MAKE MY HEAD SPIN.
NOT AT ALL! THESE ARE VERY SMART GIRLS. AND GOOD DETECTIVES!
WELL, I ADMIT THAT THE CLUE CREW IS CERTAINLY DEDICATED. ≥SIGH≤ IT CAN GET... ***EXHAUSTING.***
BUT, IN A ***GOOD*** WAY, RIGHT?
COOL BOWL. DID THE MUSEUM GIVE YOU A SPECIAL ONE FOR BEING AN ARTIST?
NO, IT IS MINE. THE ONLY THINGS I AM ALLOWED TO OWN ARE THREE ROBES AND THIS BOWL AND...
CHOPSTICKS!

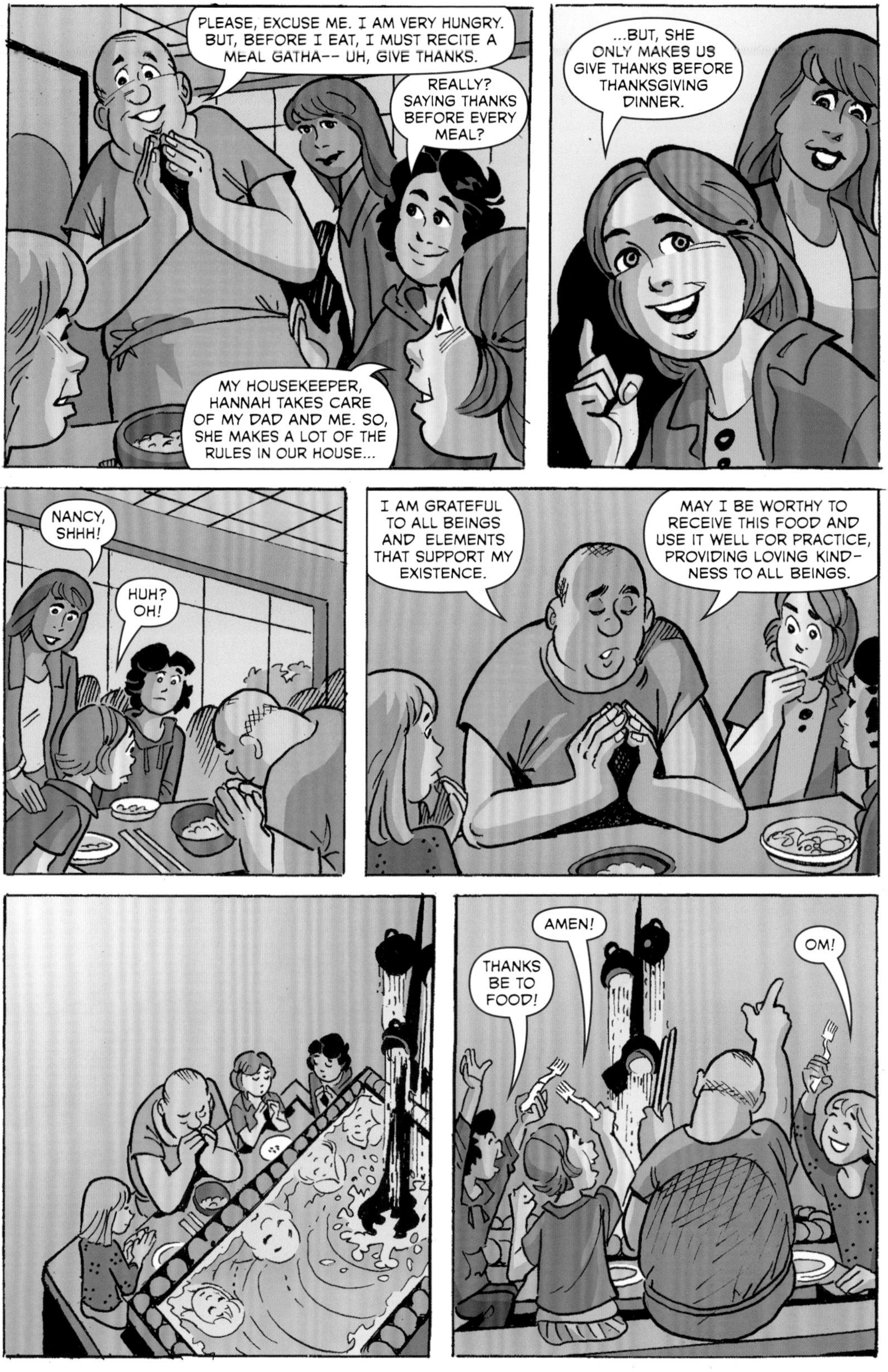
PLEASE, EXCUSE ME. I AM VERY HUNGRY. BUT, BEFORE I EAT, I MUST RECITE A MEAL GATHA-- UH, GIVE THANKS.
REALLY? SAYING THANKS BEFORE EVERY MEAL?
MY HOUSEKEEPER, HANNAH TAKES CARE OF MY DAD AND ME. SO, SHE MAKES A LOT OF THE RULES IN OUR HOUSE...
...BUT, SHE ONLY MAKES US GIVE THANKS BEFORE THANKSGIVING DINNER.
NANCY, SHHH!
HUH? OH!
I AM GRATEFUL TO ALL BEINGS AND ELEMENTS THAT SUPPORT MY EXISTENCE.
MAY I BE WORTHY TO RECEIVE THIS FOOD AND USE IT WELL FOR PRACTICE, PROVIDING LOVING KINDNESS TO ALL BEINGS.
THANKS BE TO FOOD!
AMEN!
OM!

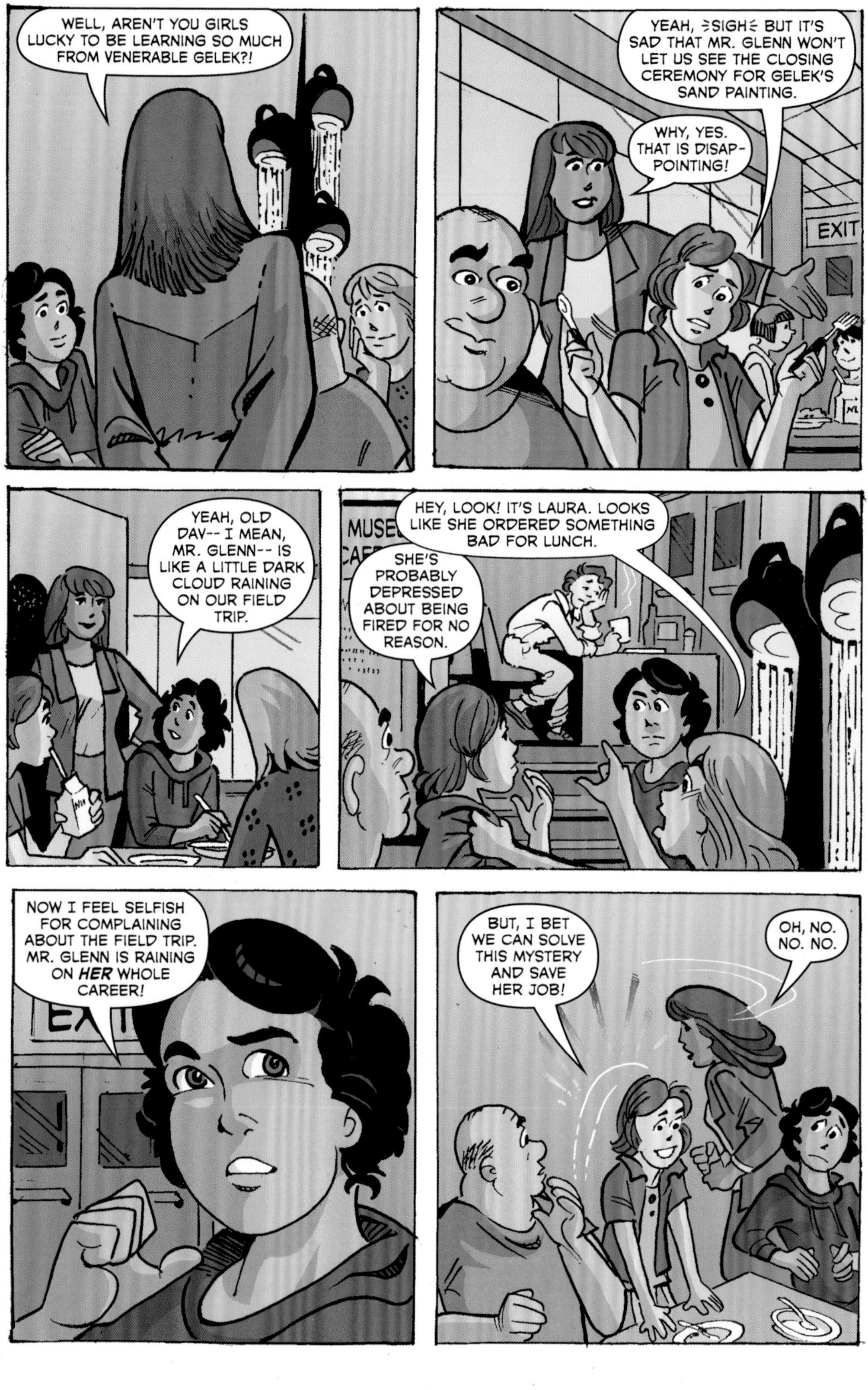
WELL, AREN'T YOU GIRLS LUCKY TO BE LEARNING SO MUCH FROM VENERABLE GELEK?!
YEAH, ⇒SIGH⇐ BUT IT'S SAD THAT MR. GLENN WON'T LET US SEE THE CLOSING CEREMONY FOR GELEK'S SAND PAINTING.
WHY, YES. THAT IS DISAP-POINTING!
EXIT
YEAH, OLD DAV-- I MEAN, MR. GLENN-- IS LIKE A LITTLE DARK CLOUD RAINING ON OUR FIELD TRIP.
HEY, LOOK! IT'S LAURA. LOOKS LIKE SHE ORDERED SOMETHING BAD FOR LUNCH.
SHE'S PROBABLY DEPRESSED ABOUT BEING FIRED FOR NO REASON.
NOW I FEEL SELFISH FOR COMPLAINING ABOUT THE FIELD TRIP. MR. GLENN IS RAINING ON *HER* WHOLE CAREER!
BUT, I BET WE CAN SOLVE THIS MYSTERY AND SAVE HER JOB!
OH, NO. NO. NO.

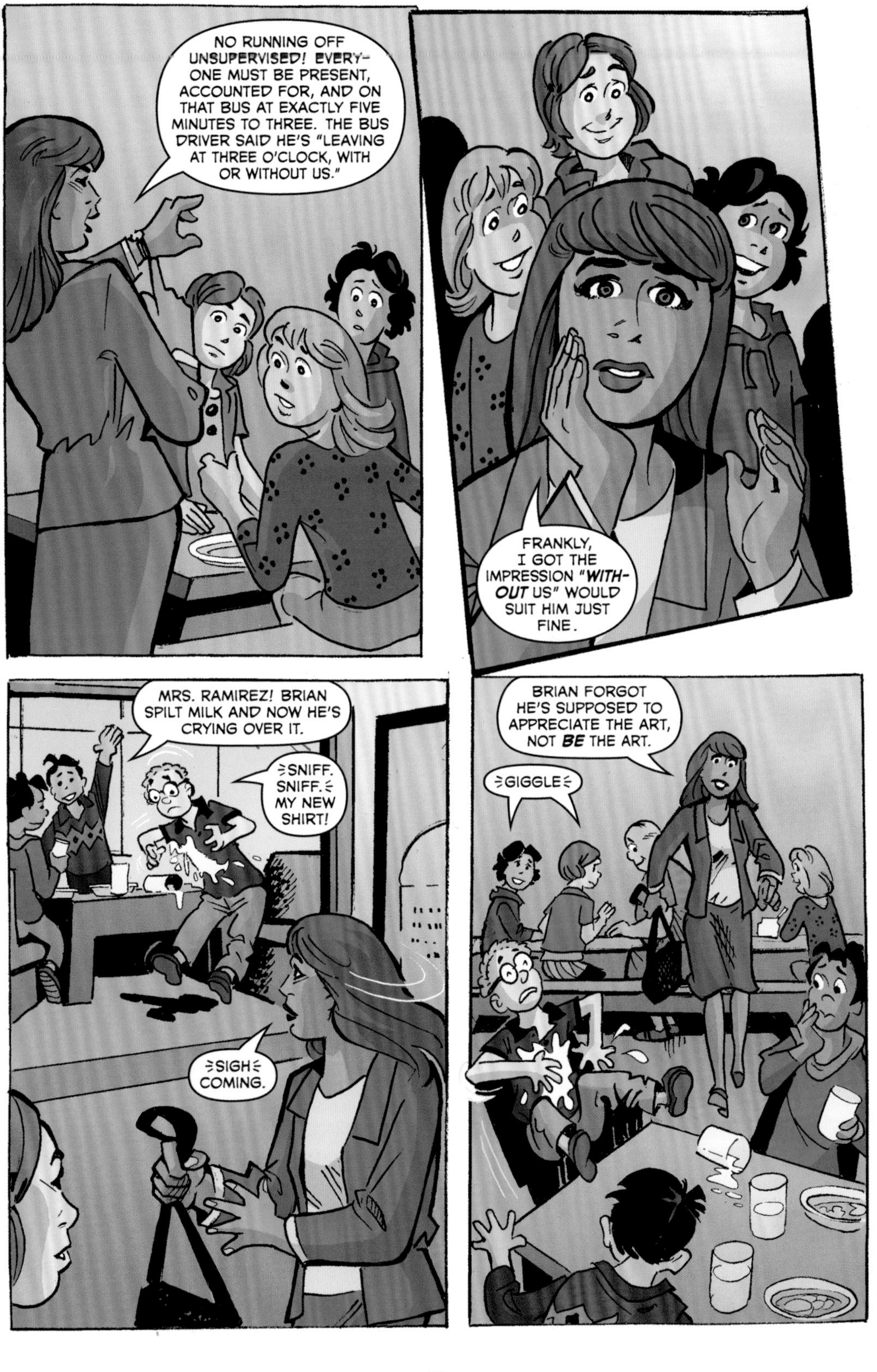
NO RUNNING OFF UNSUPERVISED! EVERY-ONE MUST BE PRESENT, ACCOUNTED FOR, AND ON THAT BUS AT EXACTLY FIVE MINUTES TO THREE. THE BUS DRIVER SAID HE'S "LEAVING AT THREE O'CLOCK, WITH OR WITHOUT US."
FRANKLY, I GOT THE IMPRESSION "*WITH-OUT* US" WOULD SUIT HIM JUST FINE.
MRS. RAMIREZ! BRIAN SPILT MILK AND NOW HE'S CRYING OVER IT.
SNIFF. SNIFF. MY NEW SHIRT!
SIGH COMING.
BRIAN FORGOT HE'S SUPPOSED TO APPRECIATE THE ART, NOT *BE* THE ART.
GIGGLE

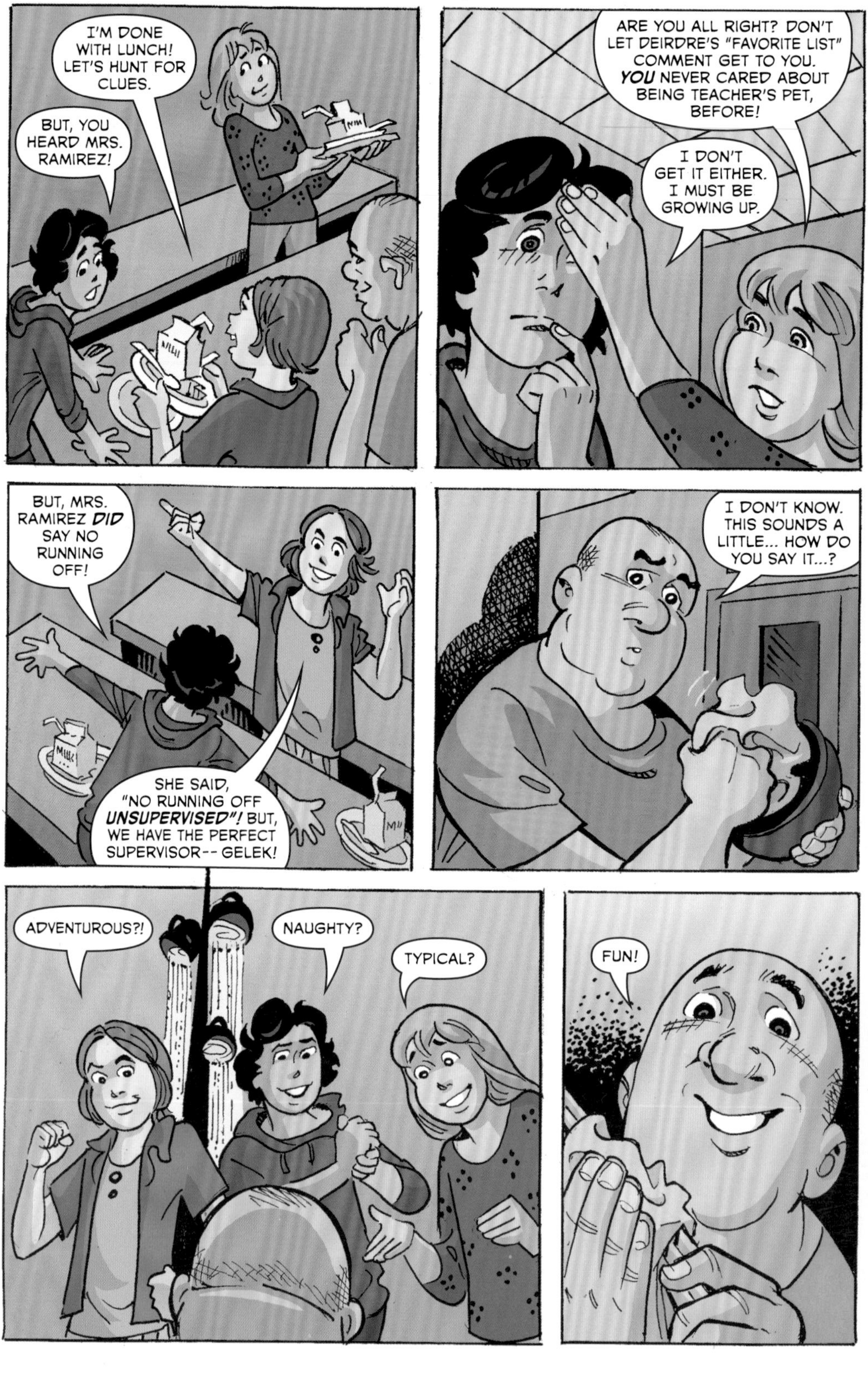
I'M DONE WITH LUNCH! LET'S HUNT FOR CLUES.
BUT, YOU HEARD MRS. RAMIREZ!
ARE YOU ALL RIGHT? DON'T LET DEIRDRE'S "FAVORITE LIST" COMMENT GET TO YOU. YOU NEVER CARED ABOUT BEING TEACHER'S PET, BEFORE!
I DON'T GET IT EITHER. I MUST BE GROWING UP.
BUT, MRS. RAMIREZ DID SAY NO RUNNING OFF!
SHE SAID, "NO RUNNING OFF UNSUPERVISED"! BUT, WE HAVE THE PERFECT SUPERVISOR-- GELEK!
I DON'T KNOW. THIS SOUNDS A LITTLE... HOW DO YOU SAY IT...?
ADVENTUROUS?!
NAUGHTY?
TYPICAL?
FUN!

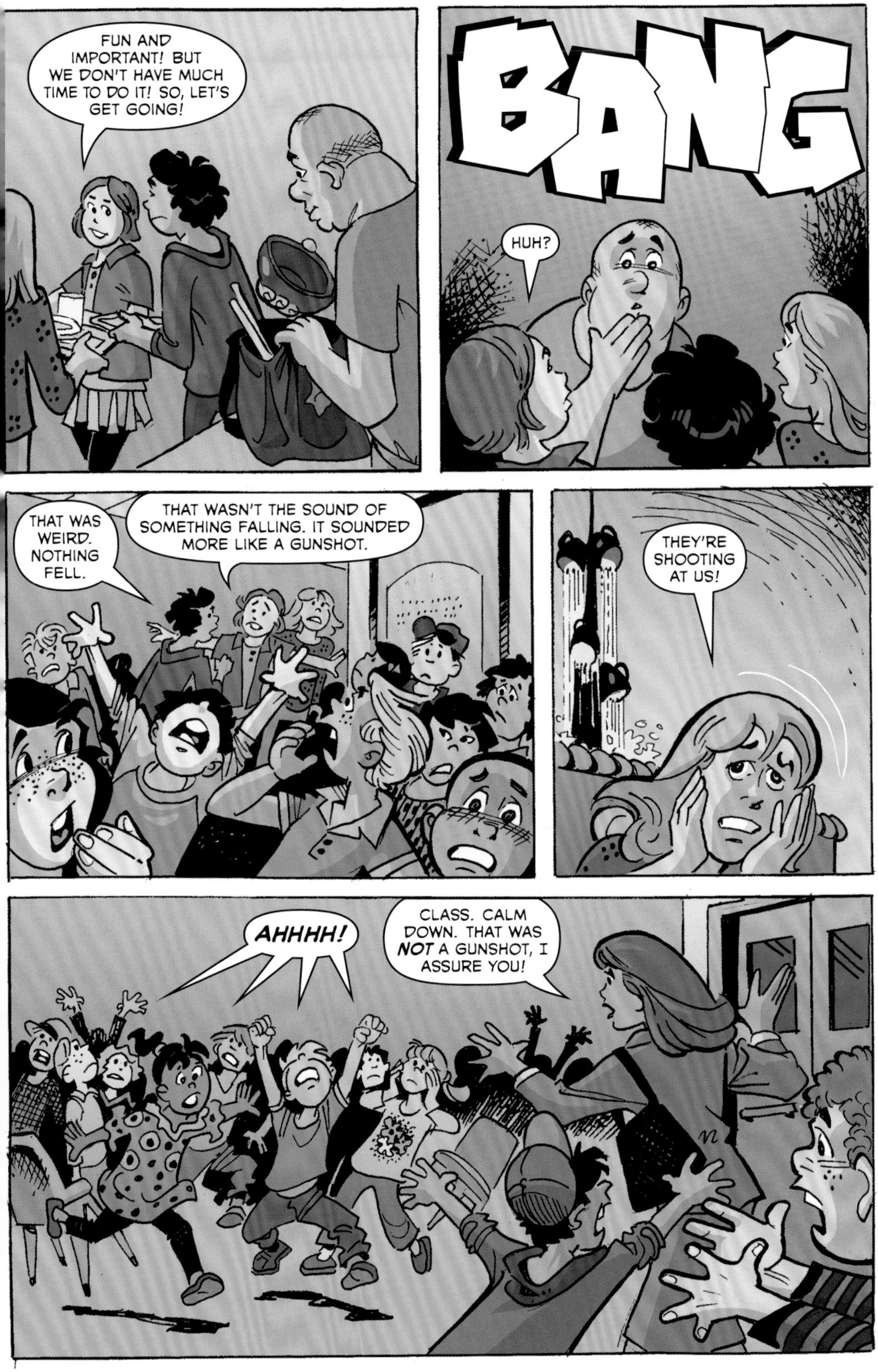
FUN AND IMPORTANT! BUT WE DON'T HAVE MUCH TIME TO DO IT! SO, LET'S GET GOING!
BANG
HUH?
THAT WAS WEIRD. NOTHING FELL.
THAT WASN'T THE SOUND OF SOMETHING FALLING. IT SOUNDED MORE LIKE A GUNSHOT.
THEY'RE SHOOTING AT US!
AHHHH!
CLASS. CALM DOWN. THAT WAS NOT A GUNSHOT, I ASSURE YOU!

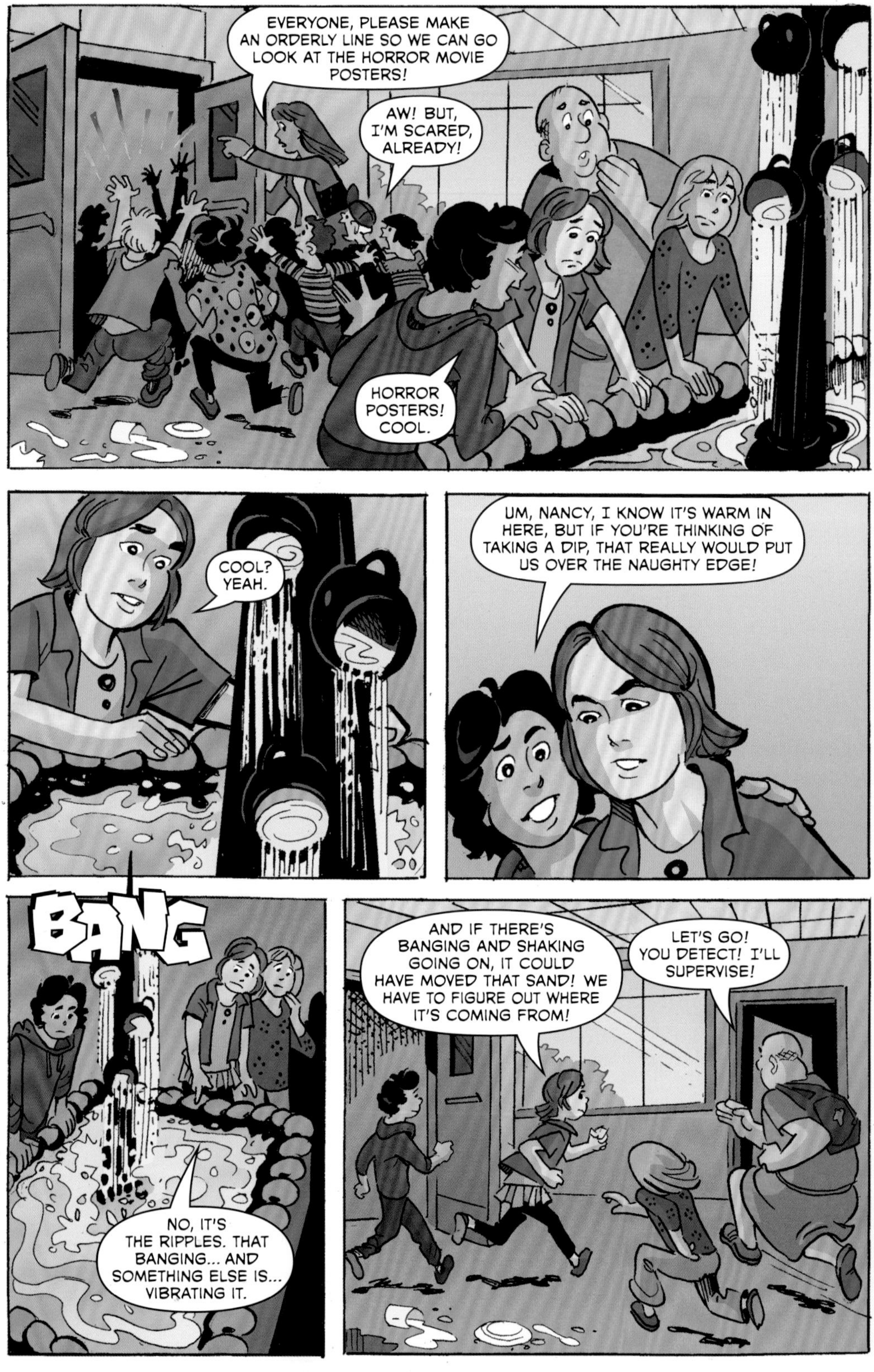
EVERYONE, PLEASE MAKE AN ORDERLY LINE SO WE CAN GO LOOK AT THE HORROR MOVIE POSTERS!
AW! BUT, I'M SCARED, ALREADY!
HORROR POSTERS! COOL.
COOL? YEAH.
UM, NANCY, I KNOW IT'S WARM IN HERE, BUT IF YOU'RE THINKING OF TAKING A DIP, THAT REALLY WOULD PUT US OVER THE NAUGHTY EDGE!
BANG
NO, IT'S THE RIPPLES. THAT BANGING... AND SOMETHING ELSE IS... VIBRATING IT.
AND IF THERE'S BANGING AND SHAKING GOING ON, IT COULD HAVE MOVED THAT SAND! WE HAVE TO FIGURE OUT WHERE IT'S COMING FROM!
LET'S GO! YOU DETECT! I'LL SUPERVISE!

CHAPTER 4: LOST AND CONFOUNDED

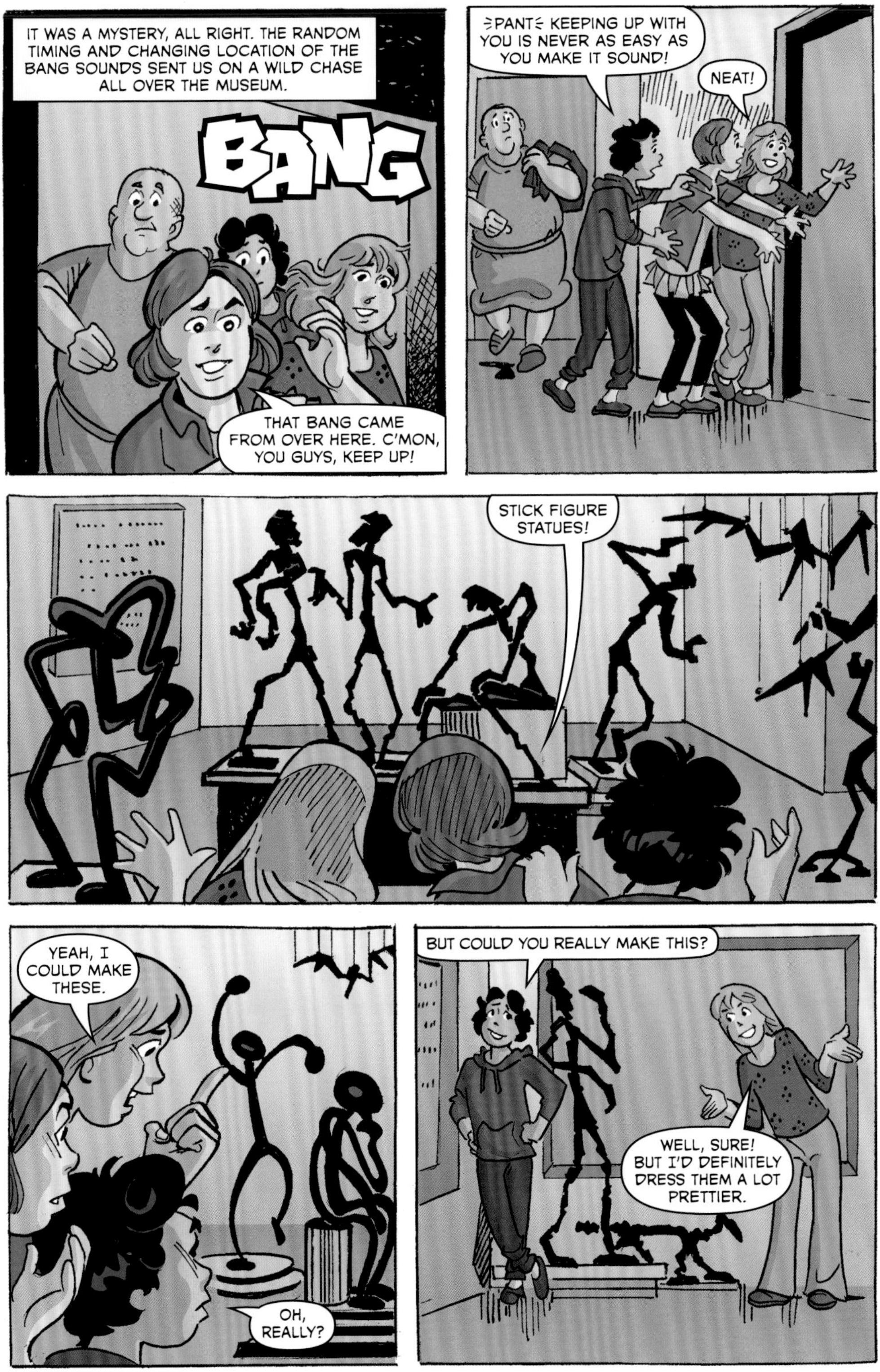
IT WAS A MYSTERY, ALL RIGHT. THE RANDOM TIMING AND CHANGING LOCATION OF THE BANG SOUNDS SENT US ON A WILD CHASE ALL OVER THE MUSEUM.
BANG
THAT BANG CAME FROM OVER HERE. C'MON, YOU GUYS, KEEP UP!
PANT KEEPING UP WITH YOU IS NEVER AS EASY AS YOU MAKE IT SOUND!
NEAT!
STICK FIGURE STATUES!
YEAH, I COULD MAKE THESE.
OH, REALLY?
BUT COULD YOU REALLY MAKE THIS?
WELL, SURE! BUT I'D DEFINITELY DRESS THEM A LOT PRETTIER.

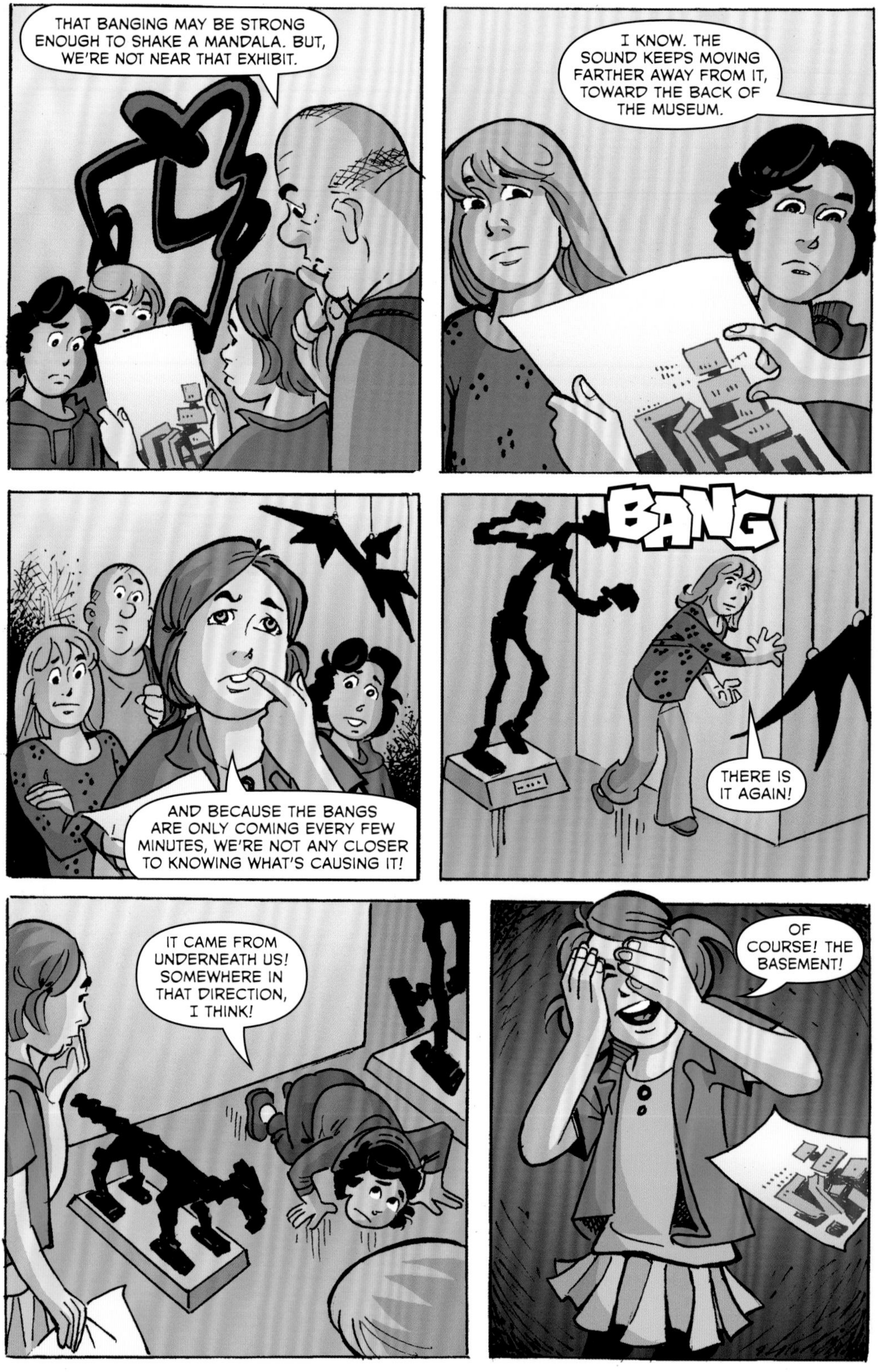

THAT BANGING MAY BE STRONG ENOUGH TO SHAKE A MANDALA. BUT, WE'RE NOT NEAR THAT EXHIBIT.
I KNOW. THE SOUND KEEPS MOVING FARTHER AWAY FROM IT, TOWARD THE BACK OF THE MUSEUM.
AND BECAUSE THE BANGS ARE ONLY COMING EVERY FEW MINUTES, WE'RE NOT ANY CLOSER TO KNOWING WHAT'S CAUSING IT!
BANG
THERE IS IT AGAIN!
IT CAME FROM UNDERNEATH US! SOMEWHERE IN THAT DIRECTION, I THINK!
OF COURSE! THE BASEMENT!

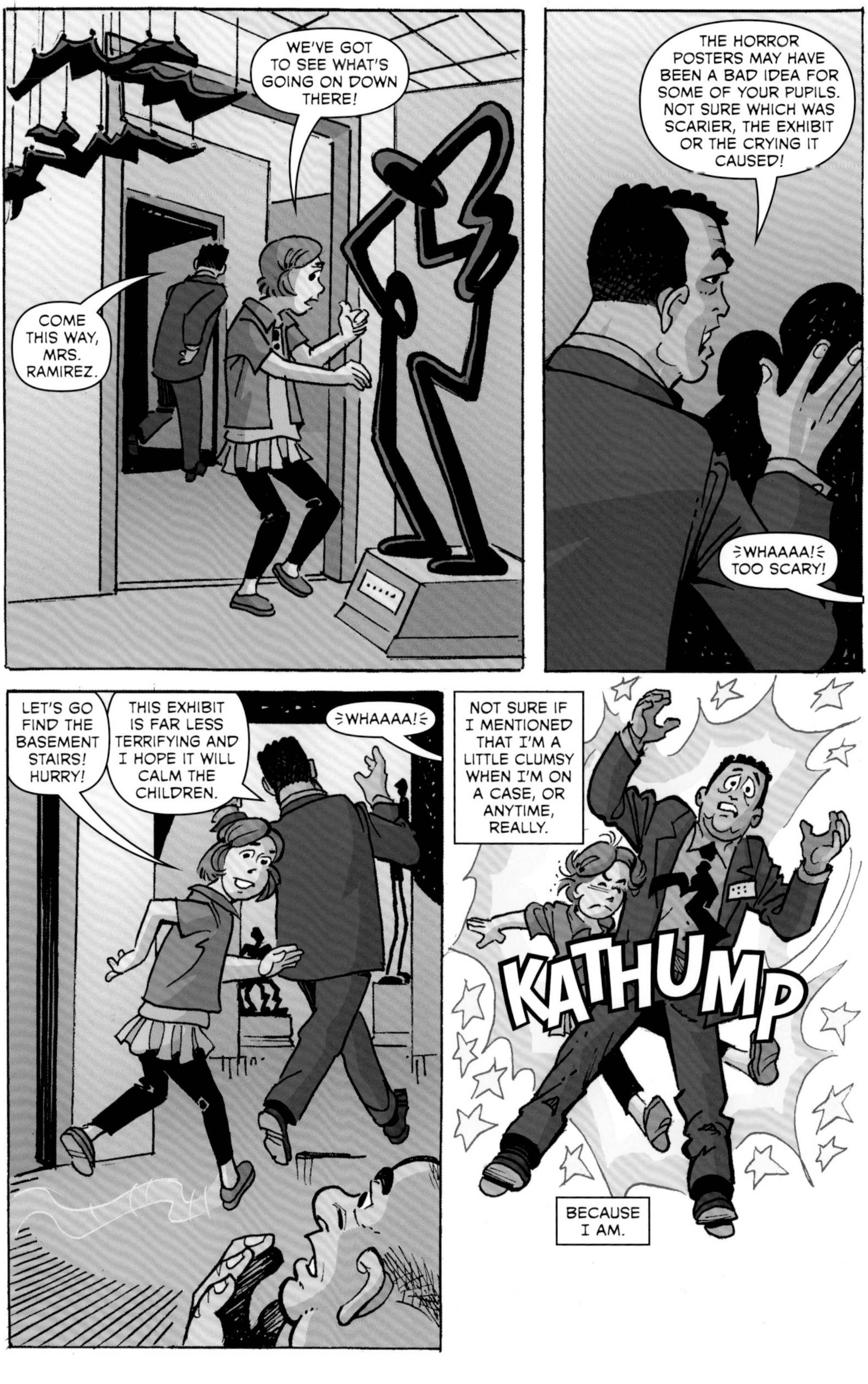
WE'VE GOT TO SEE WHAT'S GOING ON DOWN THERE!
COME THIS WAY, MRS. RAMIREZ.
THE HORROR POSTERS MAY HAVE BEEN A BAD IDEA FOR SOME OF YOUR PUPILS. NOT SURE WHICH WAS SCARIER, THE EXHIBIT OR THE CRYING IT CAUSED!
WHAAAA! TOO SCARY!
LET'S GO FIND THE BASEMENT STAIRS! HURRY!
THIS EXHIBIT IS FAR LESS TERRIFYING AND I HOPE IT WILL CALM THE CHILDREN.
WHAAAA!
NOT SURE IF I MENTIONED THAT I'M A LITTLE CLUMSY WHEN I'M ON A CASE, OR ANYTIME, REALLY.
KATHUMP
BECAUSE I AM.

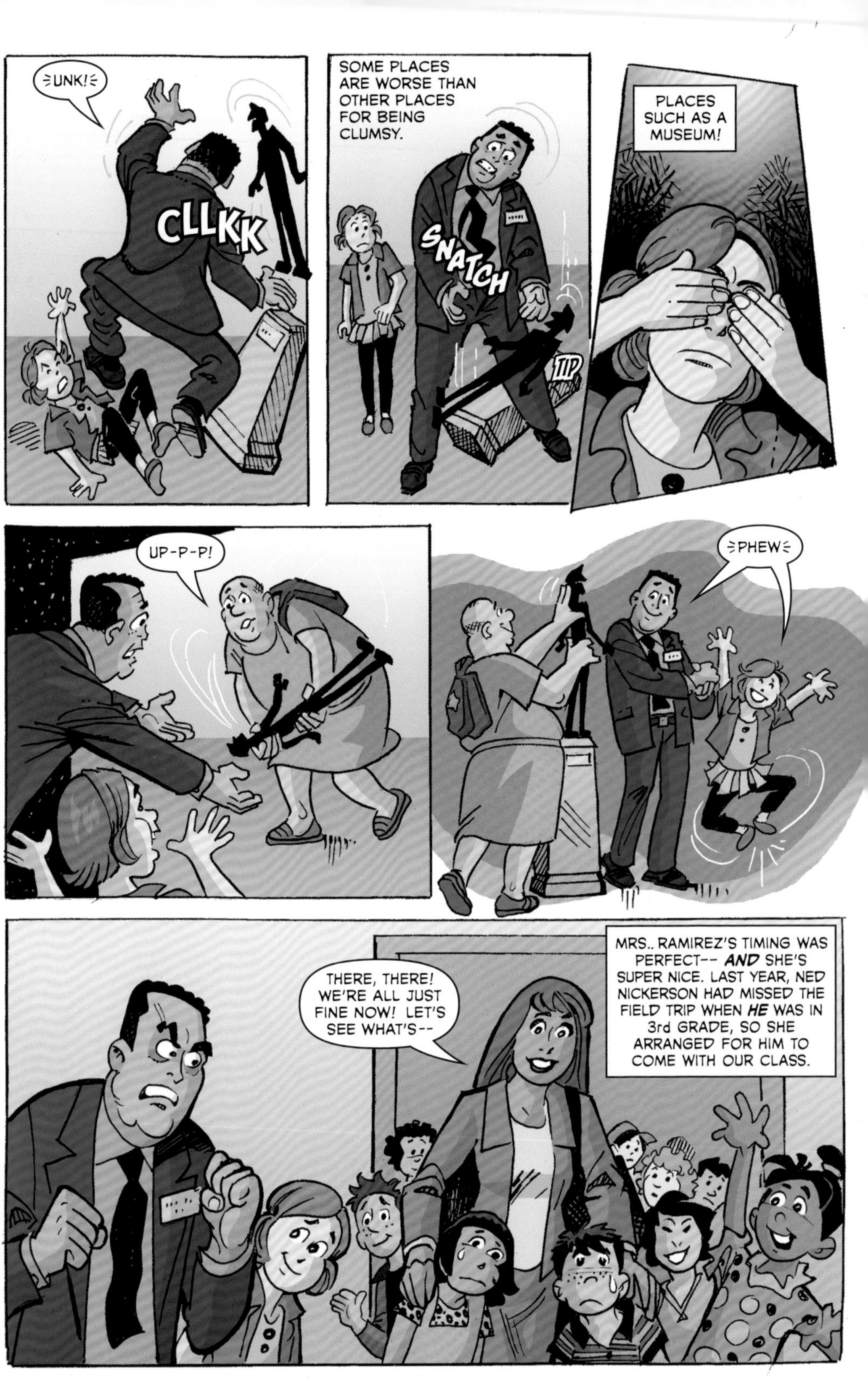
UNK!
CLLKK
SOME PLACES ARE WORSE THAN OTHER PLACES FOR BEING CLUMSY.
SNATCH
TIP
PLACES SUCH AS A MUSEUM!
UP-P-P!
PHEW
THERE, THERE! WE'RE ALL JUST FINE NOW! LET'S SEE WHAT'S--
MRS.. RAMIREZ'S TIMING WAS PERFECT-- AND SHE'S SUPER NICE. LAST YEAR, NED NICKERSON HAD MISSED THE FIELD TRIP WHEN HE WAS IN 3rd GRADE, SO SHE ARRANGED FOR HIM TO COME WITH OUR CLASS.

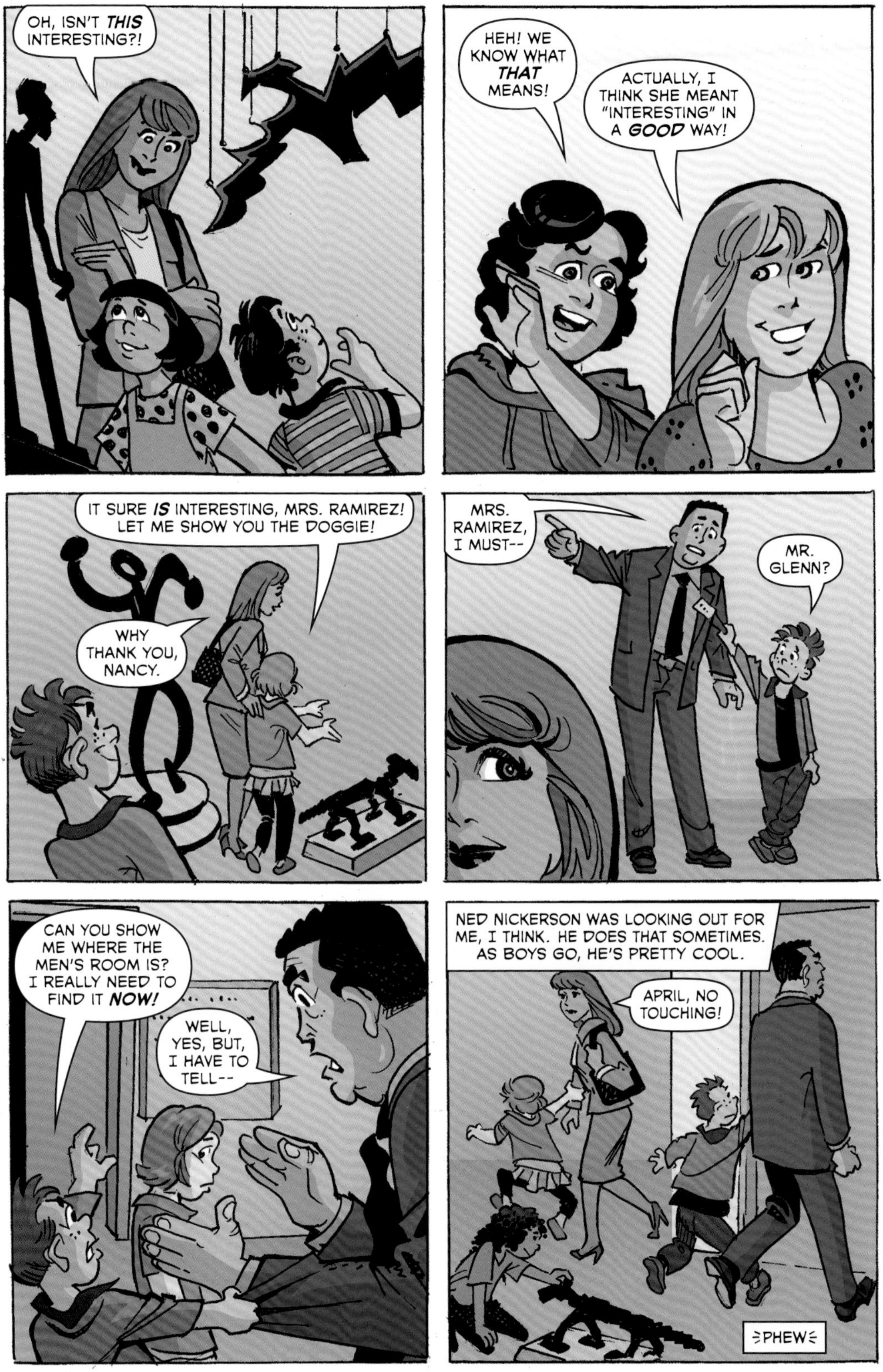
OH, ISN'T **THIS** INTERESTING?!
HEH! WE KNOW WHAT **THAT** MEANS!
ACTUALLY, I THINK SHE MEANT "INTERESTING" IN A **GOOD** WAY!
IT SURE **IS** INTERESTING, MRS. RAMIREZ! LET ME SHOW YOU THE DOGGIE!
WHY THANK YOU, NANCY.
MRS. RAMIREZ, I MUST--
MR. GLENN?
CAN YOU SHOW ME WHERE THE MEN'S ROOM IS? I REALLY NEED TO FIND IT **NOW!**
WELL, YES, BUT, I HAVE TO TELL--
NED NICKERSON WAS LOOKING OUT FOR ME, I THINK. HE DOES THAT SOMETIMES. AS BOYS GO, HE'S PRETTY COOL.
APRIL, NO TOUCHING!
PHEW

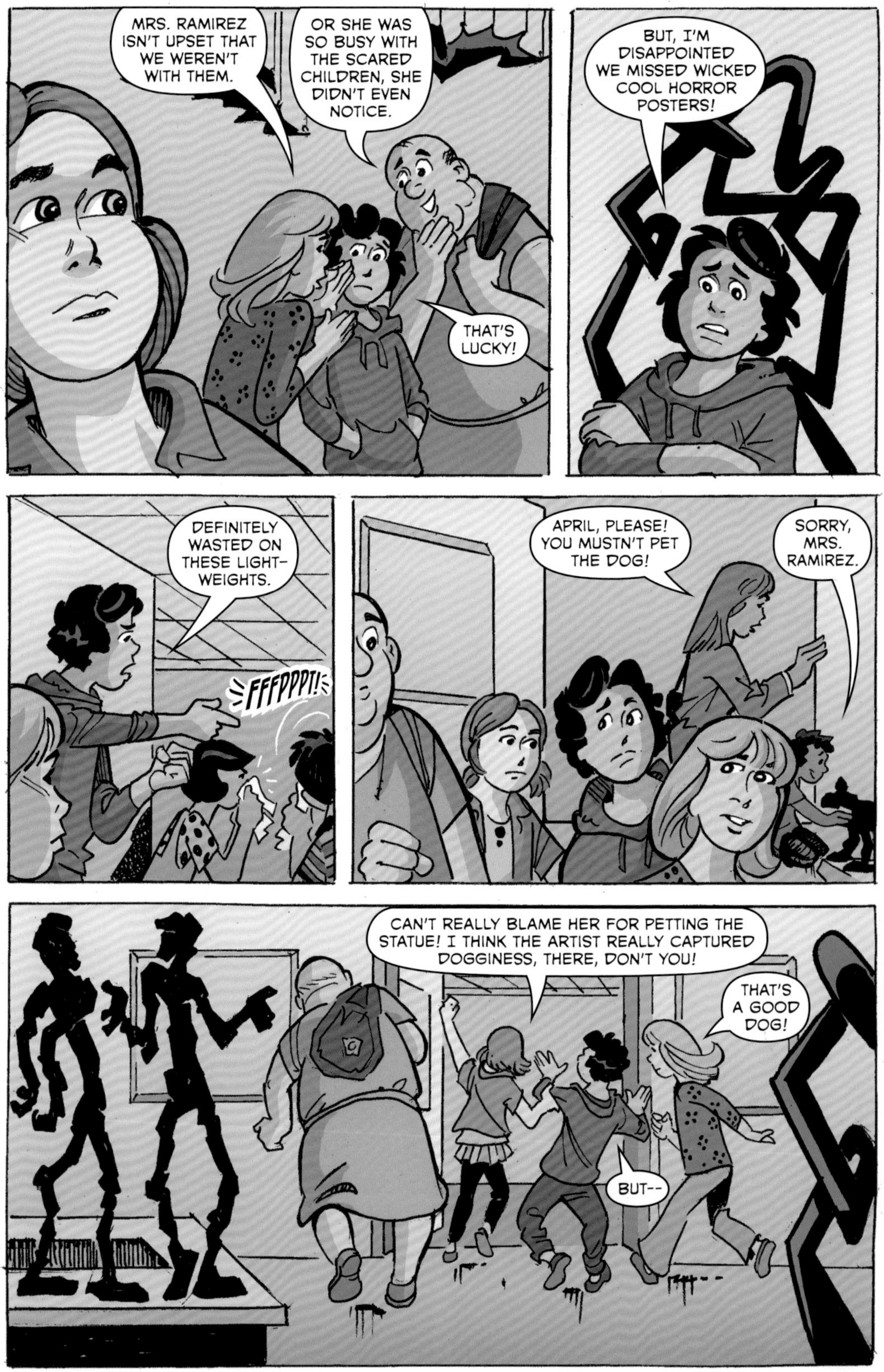
MRS. RAMIREZ ISN'T UPSET THAT WE WEREN'T WITH THEM.
OR SHE WAS SO BUSY WITH THE SCARED CHILDREN, SHE DIDN'T EVEN NOTICE.
THAT'S LUCKY!
BUT, I'M DISAPPOINTED WE MISSED WICKED COOL HORROR POSTERS!
DEFINITELY WASTED ON THESE LIGHT-WEIGHTS.
FFFPPPT!
APRIL, PLEASE! YOU MUSTN'T PET THE DOG!
SORRY, MRS. RAMIREZ.
CAN'T REALLY BLAME HER FOR PETTING THE STATUE! I THINK THE ARTIST REALLY CAPTURED DOGGINESS, THERE, DON'T YOU!
THAT'S A GOOD DOG!
BUT--

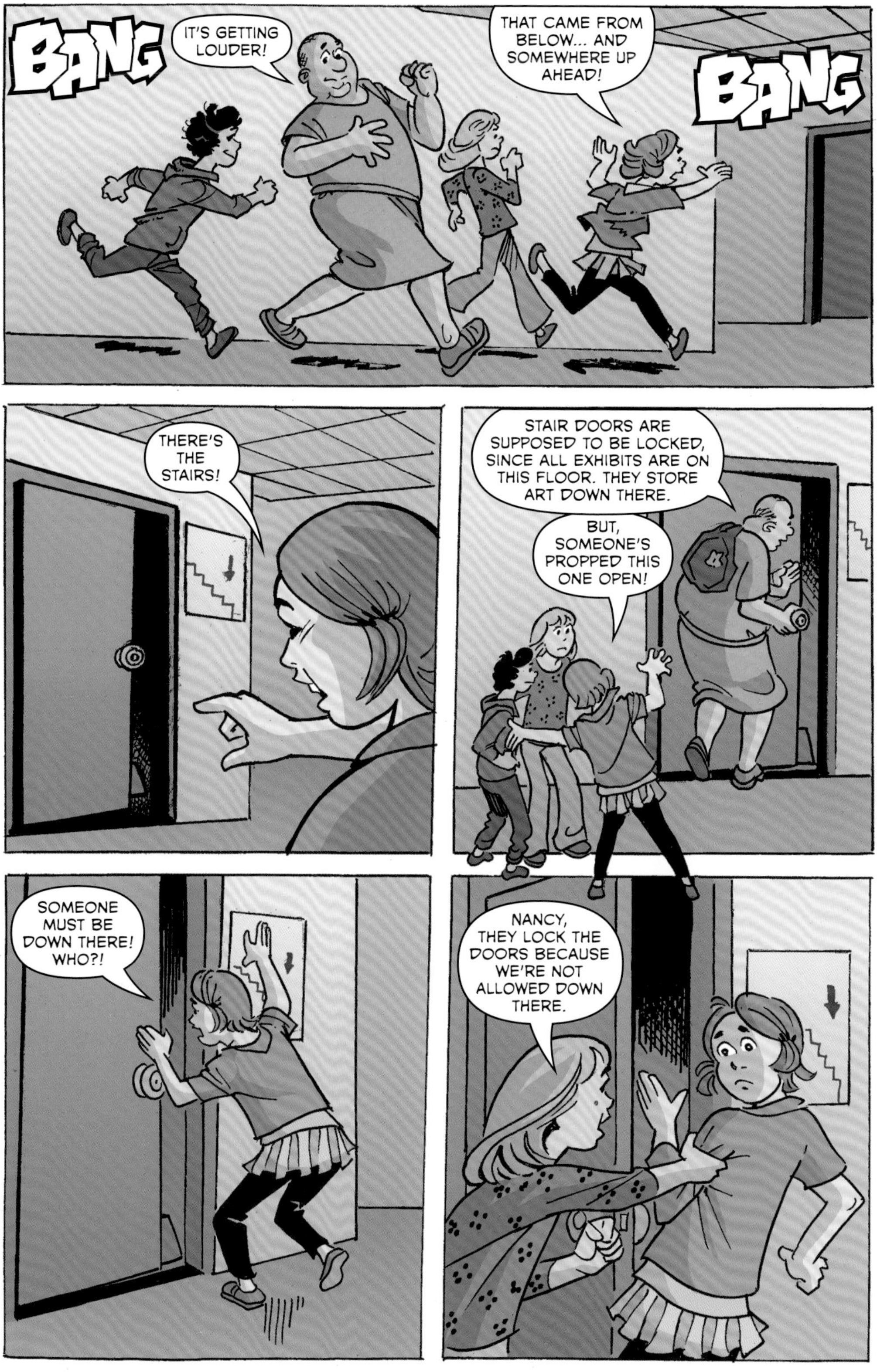
BANG
IT'S GETTING LOUDER!
THAT CAME FROM BELOW... AND SOMEWHERE UP AHEAD!
BANG
THERE'S THE STAIRS!
STAIR DOORS ARE SUPPOSED TO BE LOCKED, SINCE ALL EXHIBITS ARE ON THIS FLOOR. THEY STORE ART DOWN THERE.
BUT, SOMEONE'S PROPPED THIS ONE OPEN!
SOMEONE MUST BE DOWN THERE! WHO?!
NANCY, THEY LOCK THE DOORS BECAUSE WE'RE NOT ALLOWED DOWN THERE.

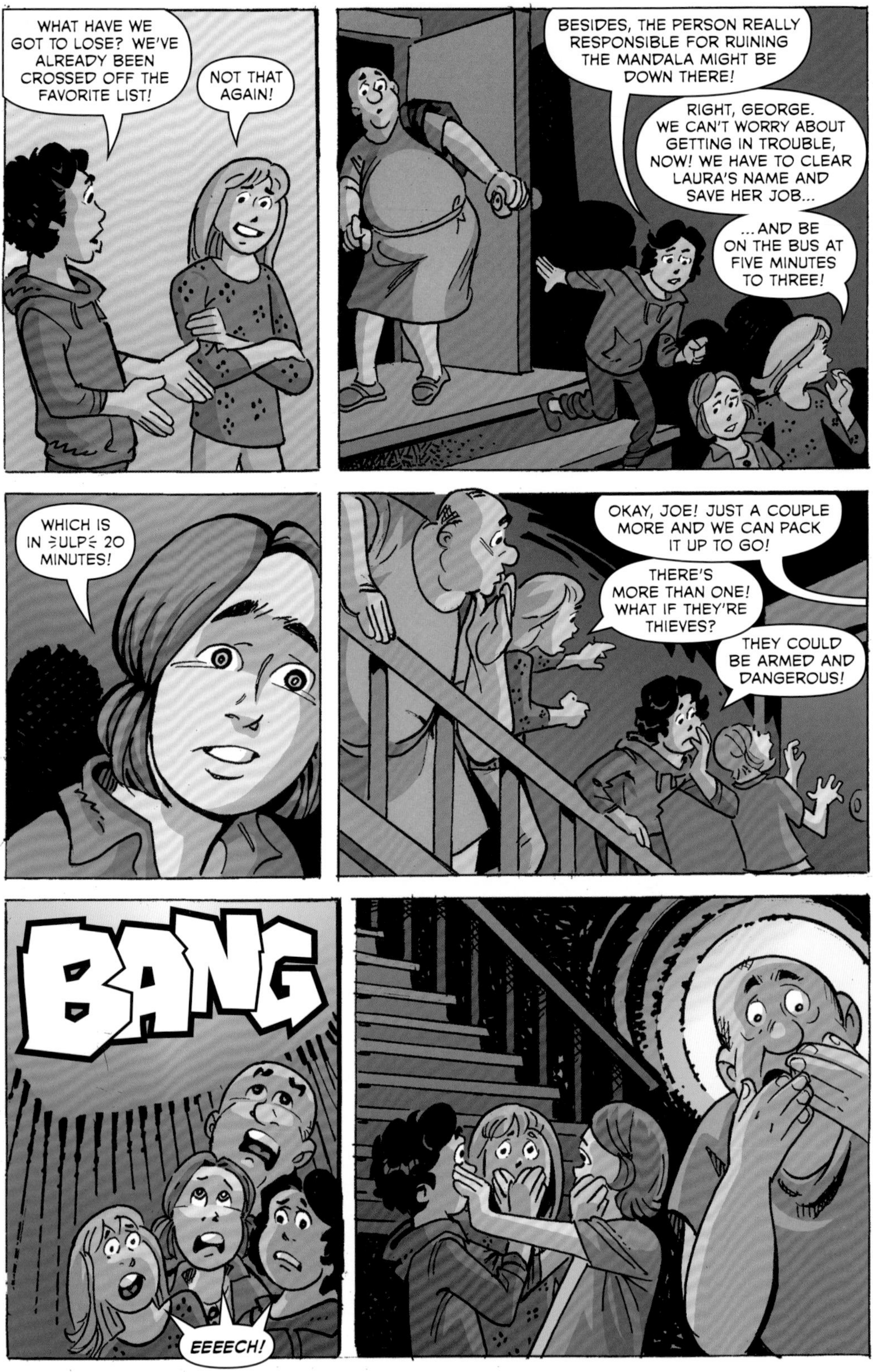
WHAT HAVE WE GOT TO LOSE? WE'VE ALREADY BEEN CROSSED OFF THE FAVORITE LIST!
NOT THAT AGAIN!
BESIDES, THE PERSON REALLY RESPONSIBLE FOR RUINING THE MANDALA MIGHT BE DOWN THERE!
RIGHT, GEORGE. WE CAN'T WORRY ABOUT GETTING IN TROUBLE, NOW! WE HAVE TO CLEAR LAURA'S NAME AND SAVE HER JOB...
...AND BE ON THE BUS AT FIVE MINUTES TO THREE!
WHICH IS IN ≥ULP≤ 20 MINUTES!
OKAY, JOE! JUST A COUPLE MORE AND WE CAN PACK IT UP TO GO!
THERE'S MORE THAN ONE! WHAT IF THEY'RE THIEVES?
THEY COULD BE ARMED AND DANGEROUS!
BANG
EEEECH!

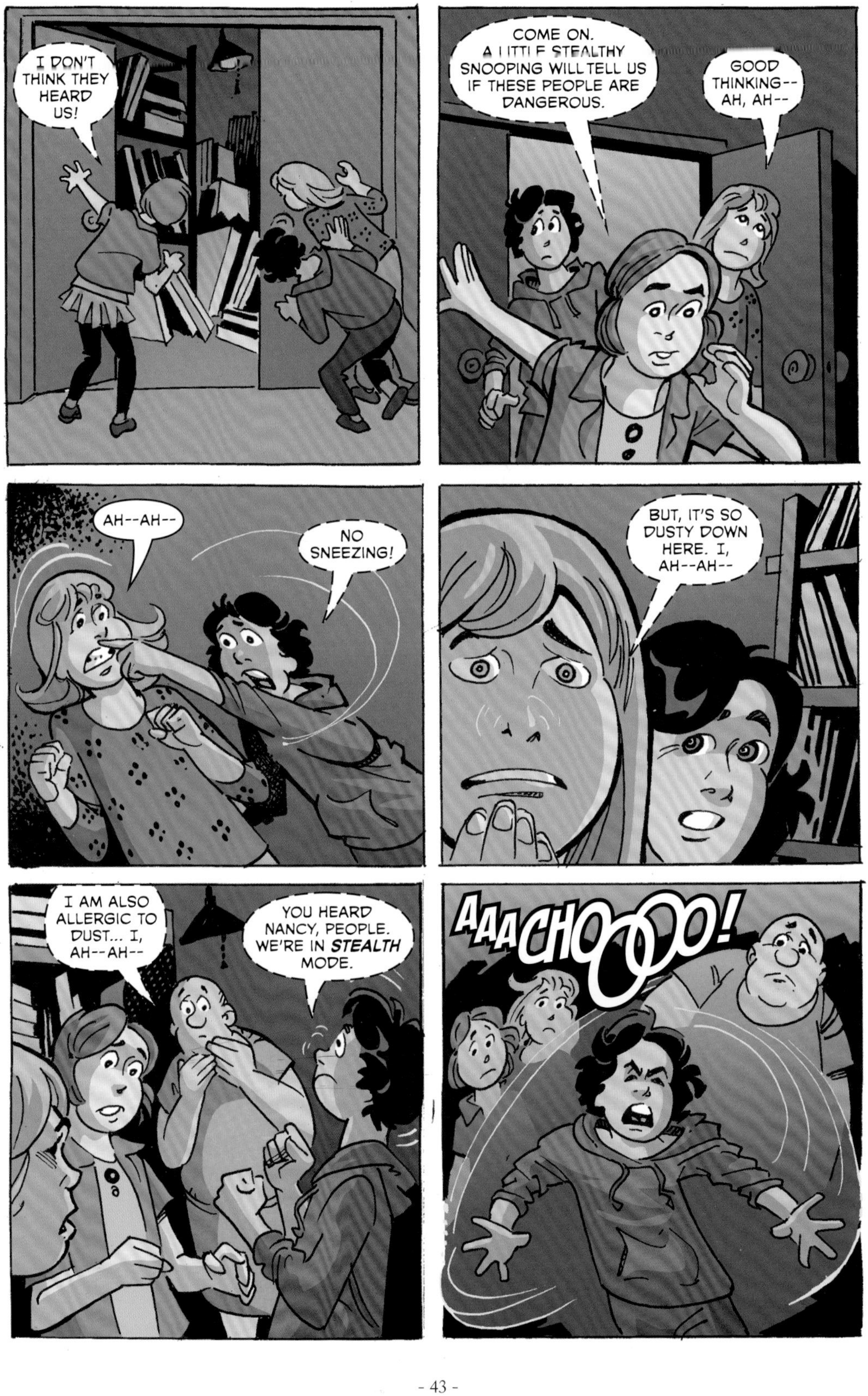
I DON'T THINK THEY HEARD US!
COME ON. A LITTLE STEALTHY SNOOPING WILL TELL US IF THESE PEOPLE ARE DANGEROUS.
GOOD THINKING-- AH, AH--
AH--AH--
NO SNEEZING!
BUT, IT'S SO DUSTY DOWN HERE. I, AH--AH--
I AM ALSO ALLERGIC TO DUST... I, AH--AH--
YOU HEARD NANCY, PEOPLE. WE'RE IN *STEALTH* MODE.
AAACHOOOOO!

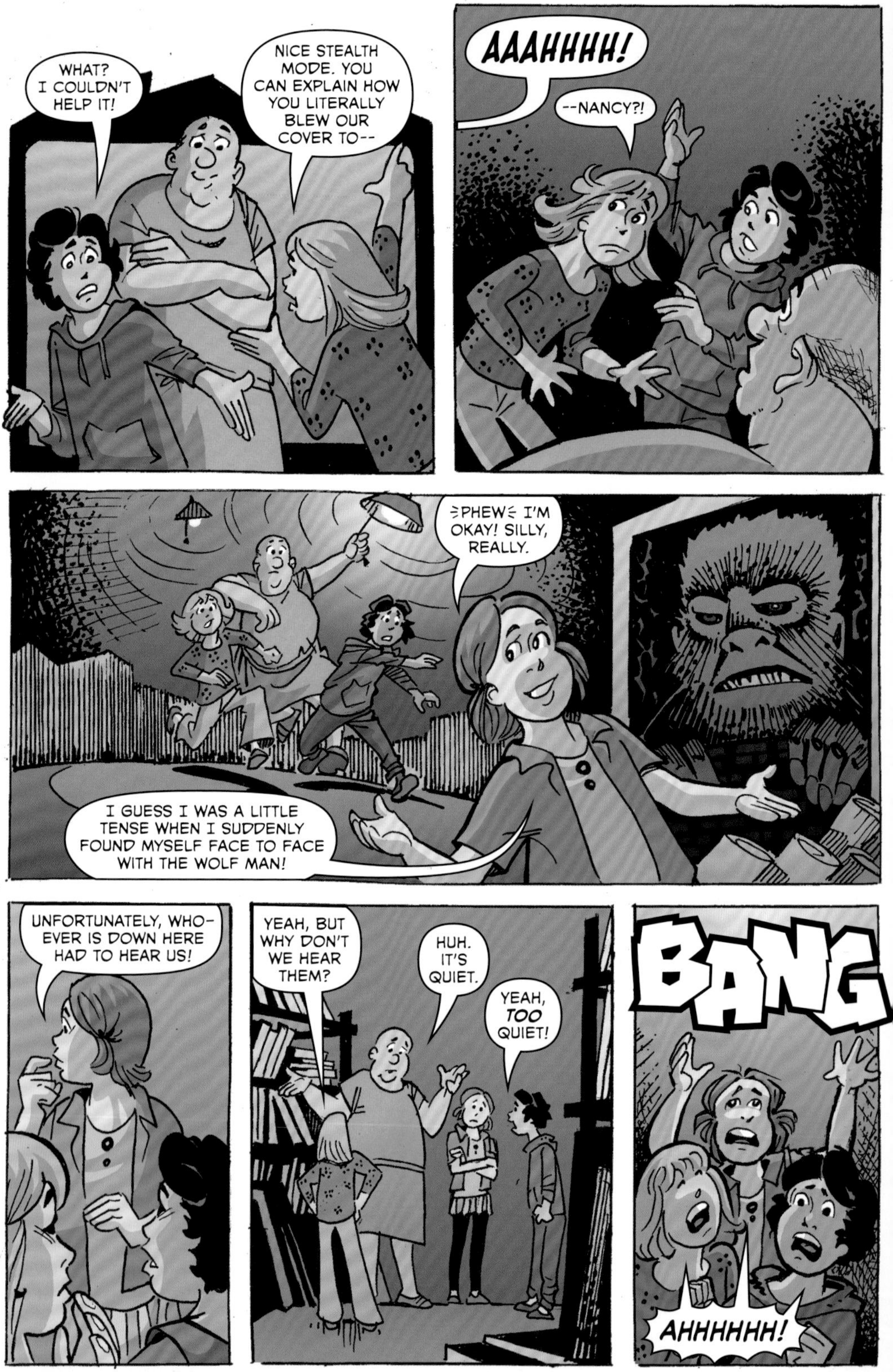
WHAT? I COULDN'T HELP IT!
NICE STEALTH MODE. YOU CAN EXPLAIN HOW YOU LITERALLY BLEW OUR COVER TO--
AAAHHHH!
--NANCY?!
PHEW I'M OKAY! SILLY, REALLY.
I GUESS I WAS A LITTLE TENSE WHEN I SUDDENLY FOUND MYSELF FACE TO FACE WITH THE WOLF MAN!
UNFORTUNATELY, WHO-EVER IS DOWN HERE HAD TO HEAR US!
YEAH, BUT WHY DON'T WE HEAR THEM?
HUH. IT'S QUIET.
YEAH, TOO QUIET!
BANG
AHHHHHH!

CHAPTER 5: THE DEVIL'S IN THE DUCTWORK

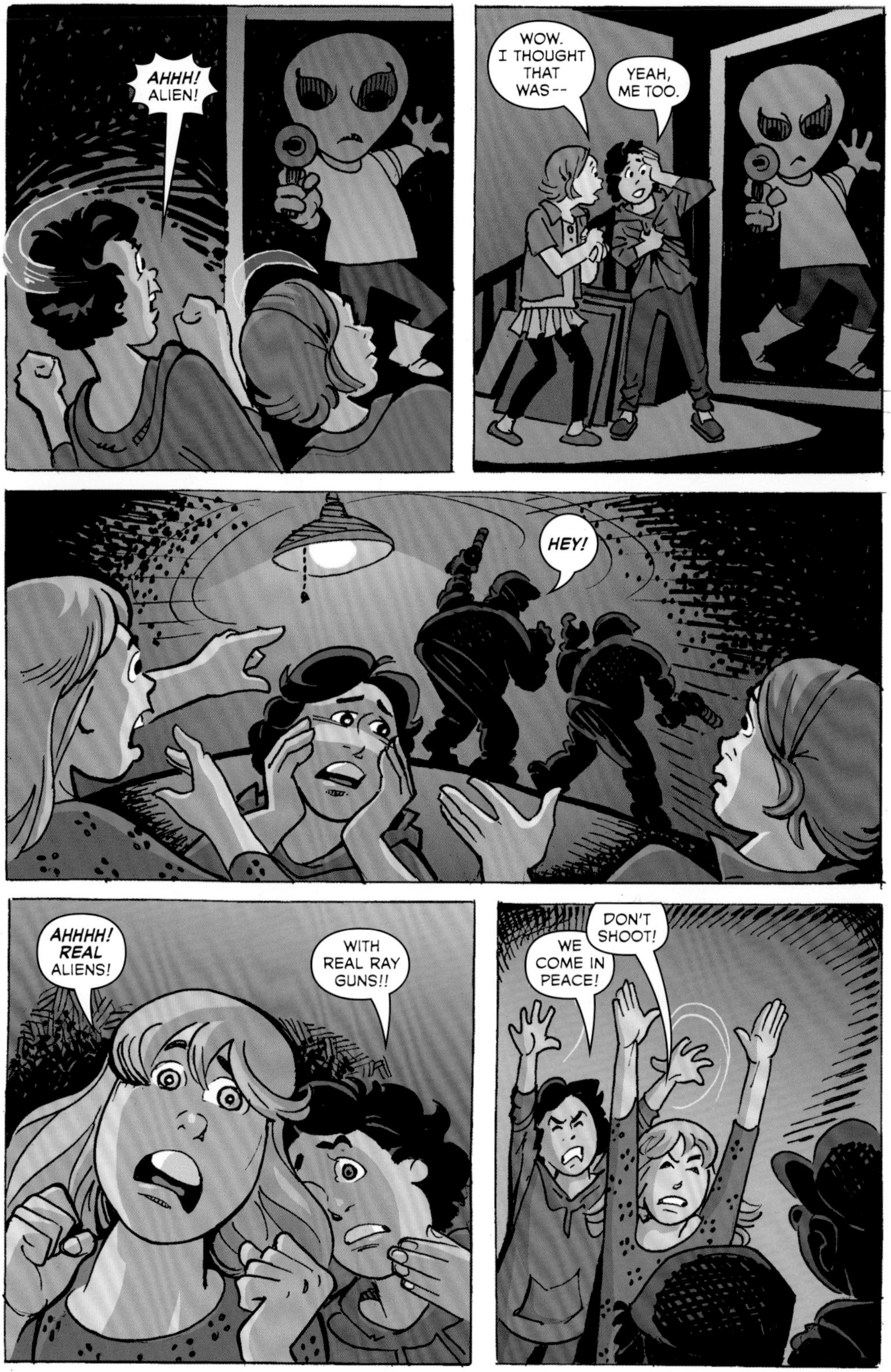

AHHH! ALIEN!
WOW. I THOUGHT THAT WAS--
YEAH, ME TOO.
HEY!
AHHHH! REAL ALIENS!
WITH REAL RAY GUNS!!
WE COME IN PEACE!
DON'T SHOOT!

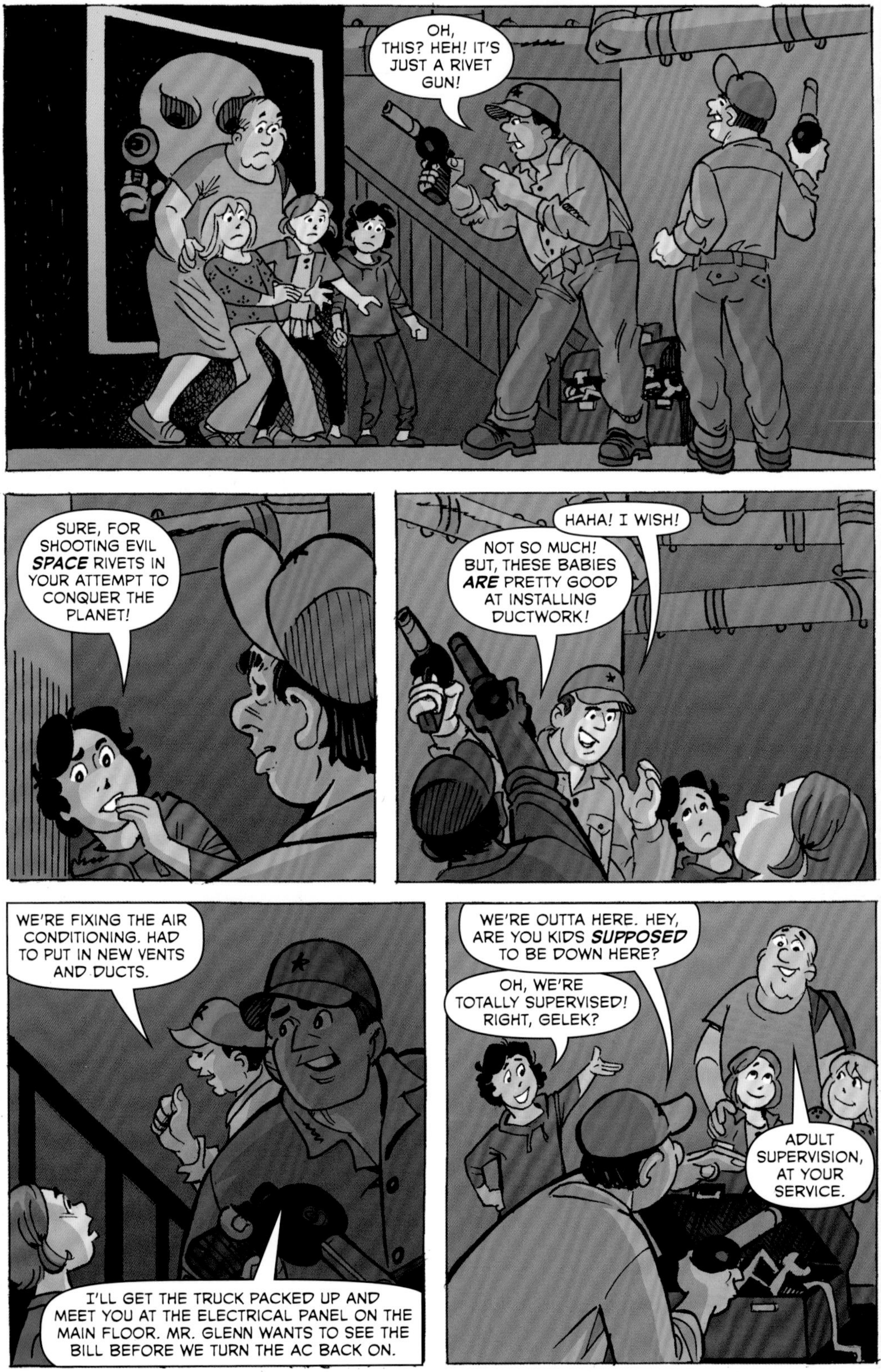

OH, THIS? HEH! IT'S JUST A RIVET GUN!
SURE, FOR SHOOTING EVIL SPACE RIVETS IN YOUR ATTEMPT TO CONQUER THE PLANET!
HAHA! I WISH!
NOT SO MUCH! BUT, THESE BABIES ARE PRETTY GOOD AT INSTALLING DUCTWORK!
WE'RE FIXING THE AIR CONDITIONING. HAD TO PUT IN NEW VENTS AND DUCTS.
I'LL GET THE TRUCK PACKED UP AND MEET YOU AT THE ELECTRICAL PANEL ON THE MAIN FLOOR. MR. GLENN WANTS TO SEE THE BILL BEFORE WE TURN THE AC BACK ON.
WE'RE OUTTA HERE. HEY, ARE YOU KIDS SUPPOSED TO BE DOWN HERE?
OH, WE'RE TOTALLY SUPERVISED! RIGHT, GELEK?
ADULT SUPERVISION, AT YOUR SERVICE.

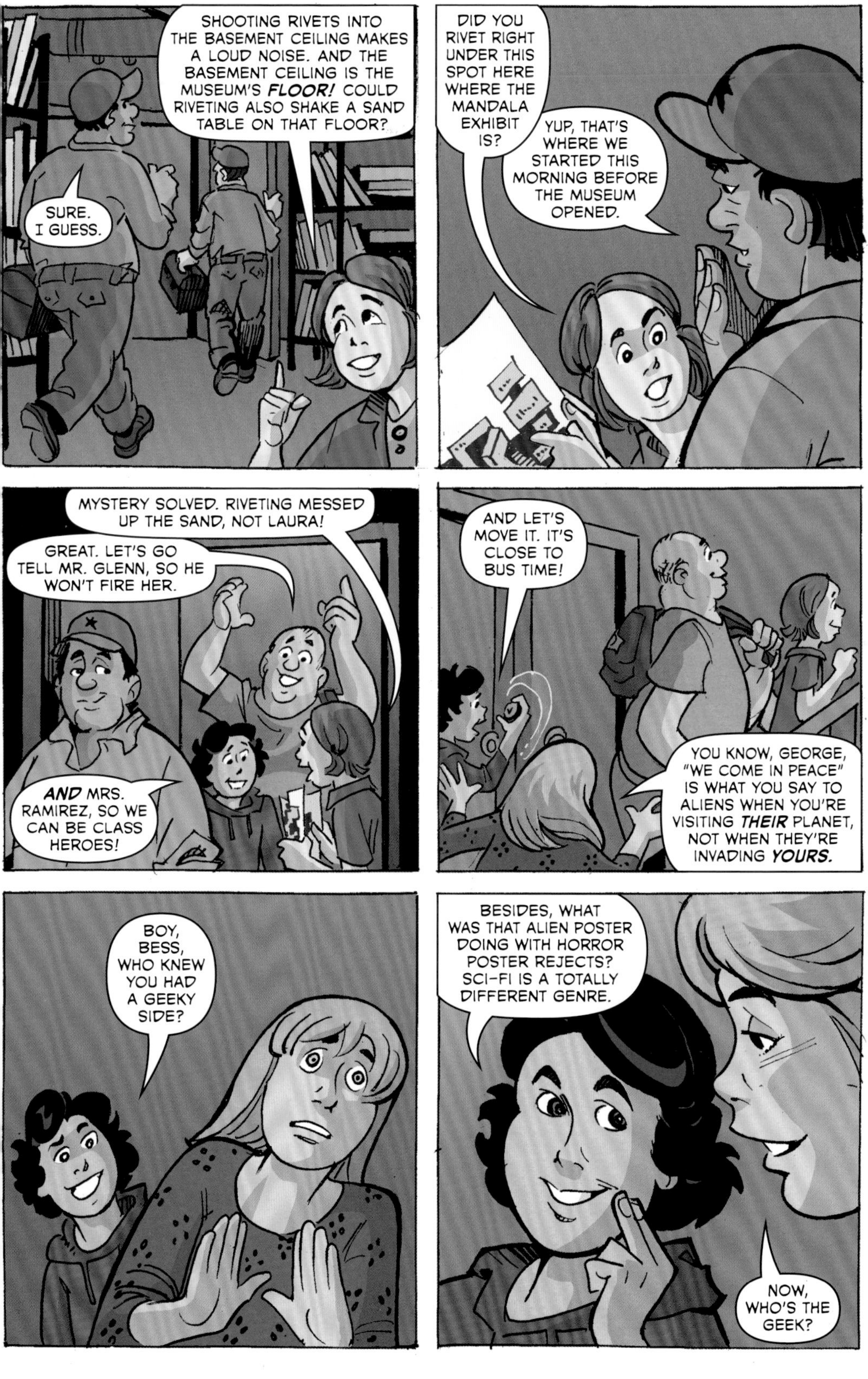
SHOOTING RIVETS INTO THE BASEMENT CEILING MAKES A LOUD NOISE. AND THE BASEMENT CEILING IS THE MUSEUM'S FLOOR! COULD RIVETING ALSO SHAKE A SAND TABLE ON THAT FLOOR?
SURE. I GUESS.
DID YOU RIVET RIGHT UNDER THIS SPOT HERE WHERE THE MANDALA EXHIBIT IS?
YUP, THAT'S WHERE WE STARTED THIS MORNING BEFORE THE MUSEUM OPENED.
MYSTERY SOLVED. RIVETING MESSED UP THE SAND, NOT LAURA!
GREAT. LET'S GO TELL MR. GLENN, SO HE WON'T FIRE HER.
AND MRS. RAMIREZ, SO WE CAN BE CLASS HEROES!
AND LET'S MOVE IT. IT'S CLOSE TO BUS TIME!
YOU KNOW, GEORGE, "WE COME IN PEACE" IS WHAT YOU SAY TO ALIENS WHEN YOU'RE VISITING THEIR PLANET, NOT WHEN THEY'RE INVADING YOURS.
BOY, BESS, WHO KNEW YOU HAD A GEEKY SIDE?
BESIDES, WHAT WAS THAT ALIEN POSTER DOING WITH HORROR POSTER REJECTS? SCI-FI IS A TOTALLY DIFFERENT GENRE.
NOW, WHO'S THE GEEK?

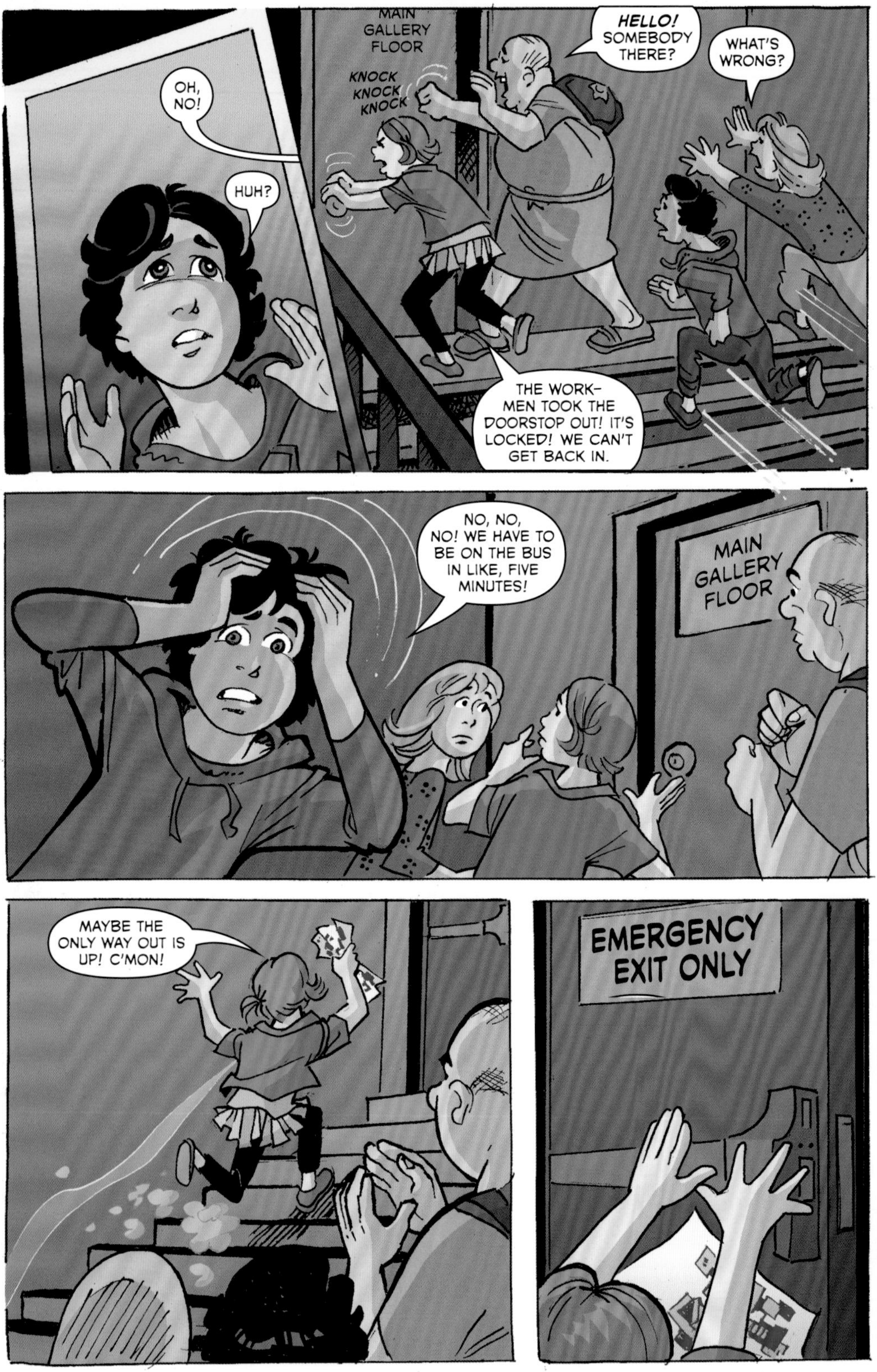
MAIN GALLERY FLOOR
KNOCK KNOCK KNOCK
HELLO! SOMEBODY THERE?
OH, NO!
WHAT'S WRONG?
HUH?
THE WORK-MEN TOOK THE DOORSTOP OUT! IT'S LOCKED! WE CAN'T GET BACK IN.
NO, NO, NO! WE HAVE TO BE ON THE BUS IN LIKE, FIVE MINUTES!
MAIN GALLERY FLOOR
MAYBE THE ONLY WAY OUT IS UP! C'MON!
EMERGENCY EXIT ONLY

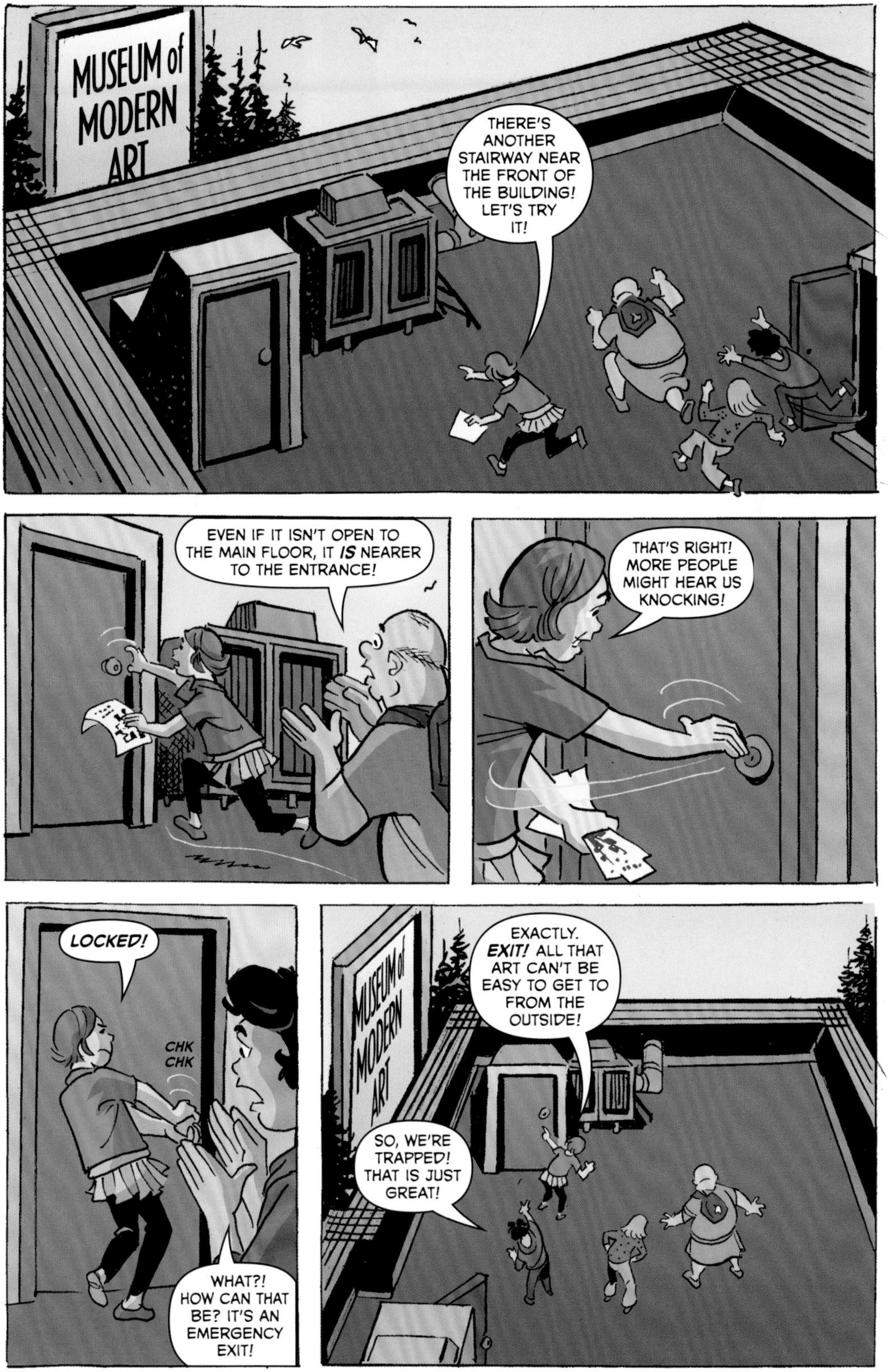
MUSEUM of MODERN ART
THERE'S ANOTHER STAIRWAY NEAR THE FRONT OF THE BUILDING! LET'S TRY IT!
EVEN IF IT ISN'T OPEN TO THE MAIN FLOOR, IT *IS* NEARER TO THE ENTRANCE!
THAT'S RIGHT! MORE PEOPLE MIGHT HEAR US KNOCKING!
LOCKED!
CHK CHK
WHAT?! HOW CAN THAT BE? IT'S AN EMERGENCY EXIT!
MUSEUM of MODERN ART
EXACTLY. *EXIT!* ALL THAT ART CAN'T BE EASY TO GET TO FROM THE OUTSIDE!
SO, WE'RE TRAPPED! THAT IS JUST GREAT!

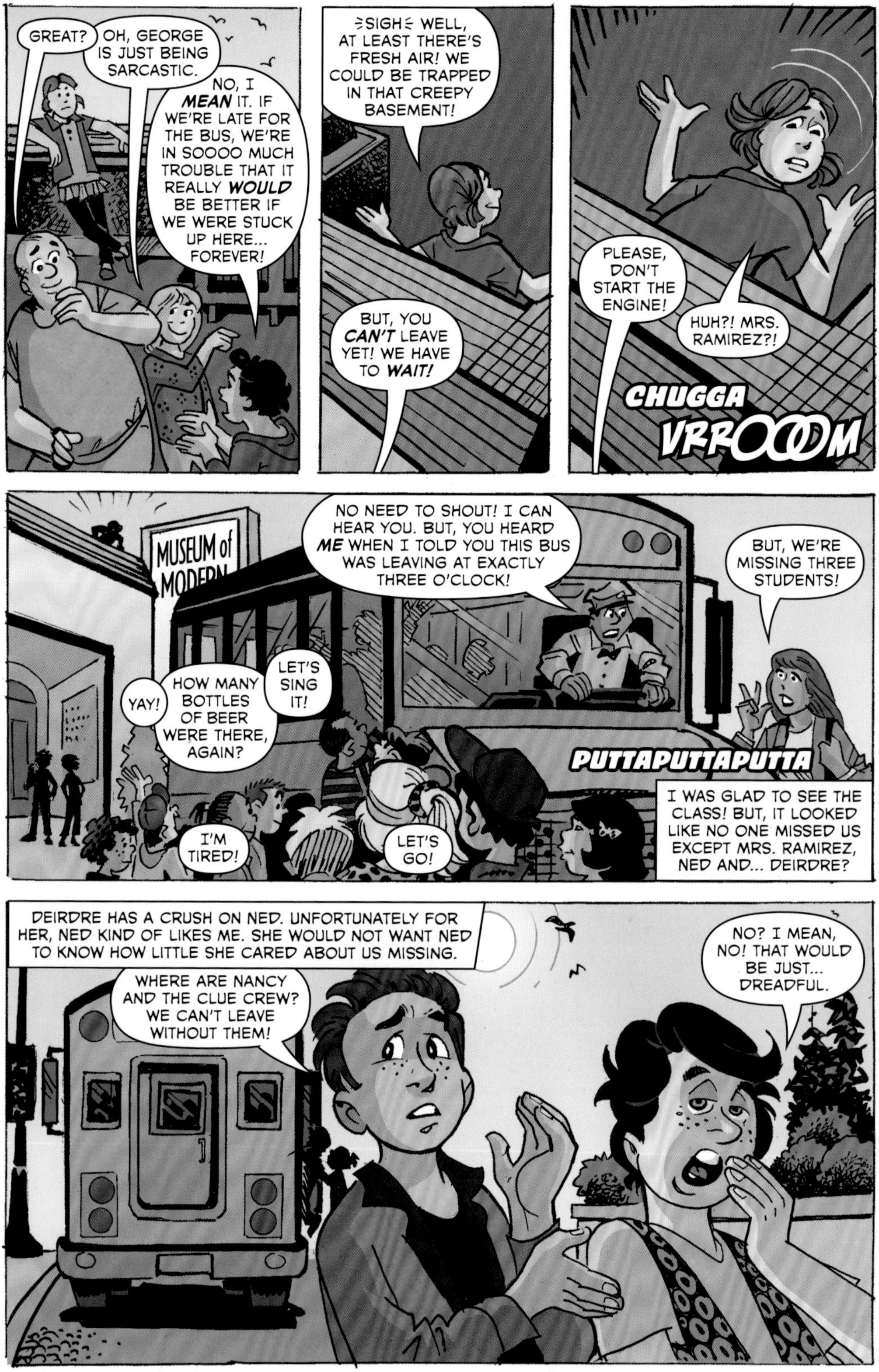
GREAT?
OH, GEORGE IS JUST BEING SARCASTIC.
NO, I MEAN IT. IF WE'RE LATE FOR THE BUS, WE'RE IN SOOOO MUCH TROUBLE THAT IT REALLY WOULD BE BETTER IF WE WERE STUCK UP HERE... FOREVER!
≡SIGH≡ WELL, AT LEAST THERE'S FRESH AIR! WE COULD BE TRAPPED IN THAT CREEPY BASEMENT!
BUT, YOU CAN'T LEAVE YET! WE HAVE TO WAIT!
PLEASE, DON'T START THE ENGINE!
HUH?! MRS. RAMIREZ?!
CHUGGA
VRROOOM
MUSEUM of MODERN
NO NEED TO SHOUT! I CAN HEAR YOU. BUT, YOU HEARD ME WHEN I TOLD YOU THIS BUS WAS LEAVING AT EXACTLY THREE O'CLOCK!
BUT, WE'RE MISSING THREE STUDENTS!
YAY!
HOW MANY BOTTLES OF BEER WERE THERE, AGAIN?
LET'S SING IT!
PUTTAPUTTAPUTTA
I'M TIRED!
LET'S GO!
I WAS GLAD TO SEE THE CLASS! BUT, IT LOOKED LIKE NO ONE MISSED US EXCEPT MRS. RAMIREZ, NED AND... DEIRDRE?
DEIRDRE HAS A CRUSH ON NED. UNFORTUNATELY FOR HER, NED KIND OF LIKES ME. SHE WOULD NOT WANT NED TO KNOW HOW LITTLE SHE CARED ABOUT US MISSING.
WHERE ARE NANCY AND THE CLUE CREW? WE CAN'T LEAVE WITHOUT THEM!
NO? I MEAN, NO! THAT WOULD BE JUST... DREADFUL.

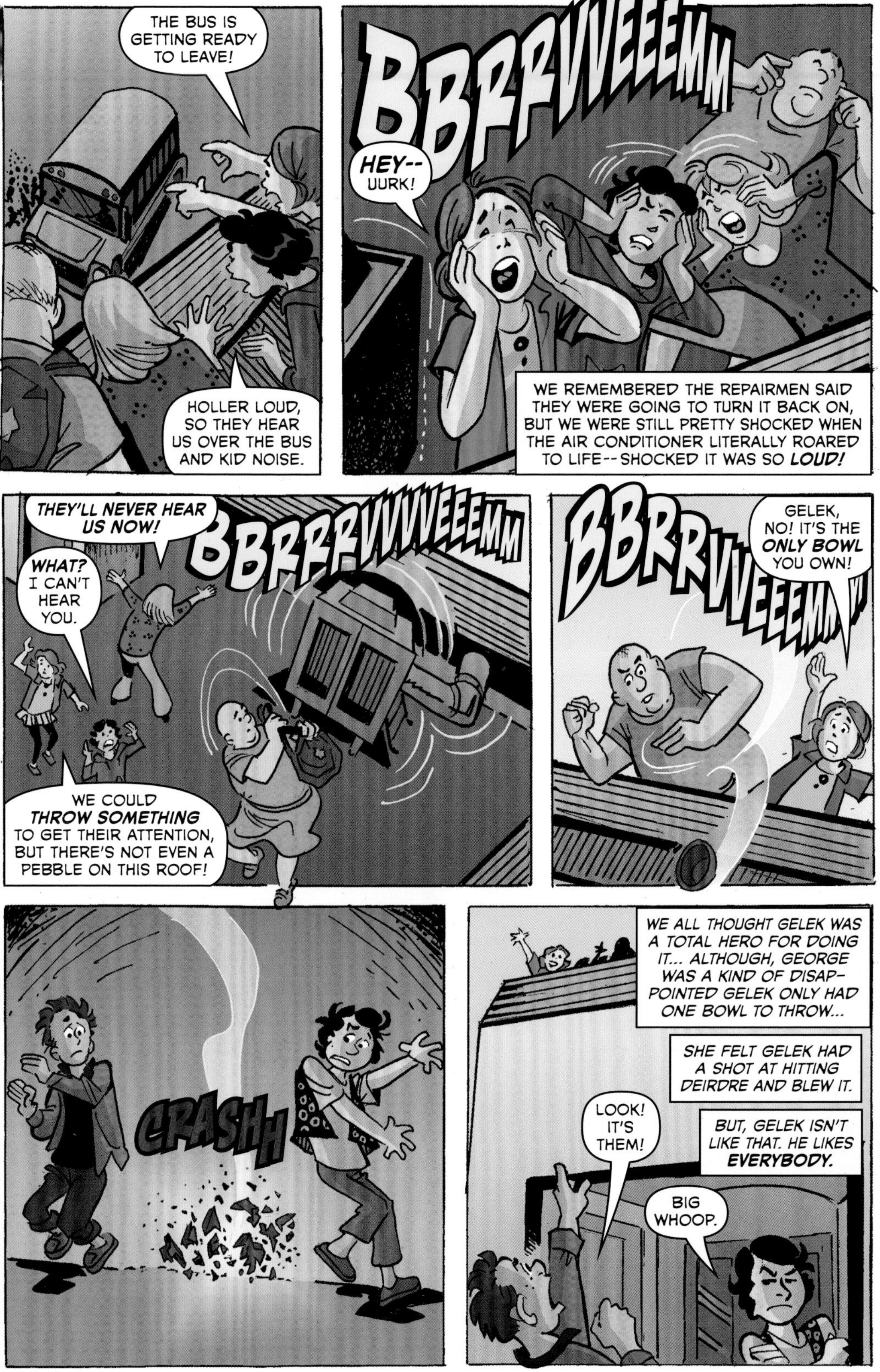
THE BUS IS GETTING READY TO LEAVE!
HOLLER LOUD, SO THEY HEAR US OVER THE BUS AND KID NOISE.
BBRRVVEEEMM
HEY-- UURK!
WE REMEMBERED THE REPAIRMEN SAID THEY WERE GOING TO TURN IT BACK ON, BUT WE WERE STILL PRETTY SHOCKED WHEN THE AIR CONDITIONER LITERALLY ROARED TO LIFE--SHOCKED IT WAS SO LOUD!
THEY'LL NEVER HEAR US NOW!
BBRRRVVVVEEEMM
WHAT? I CAN'T HEAR YOU.
WE COULD THROW SOMETHING TO GET THEIR ATTENTION, BUT THERE'S NOT EVEN A PEBBLE ON THIS ROOF!
BBRRVVEEEM
GELEK, NO! IT'S THE ONLY BOWL YOU OWN!
CRASHH
WE ALL THOUGHT GELEK WAS A TOTAL HERO FOR DOING IT... ALTHOUGH, GEORGE WAS A KIND OF DISAPPOINTED GELEK ONLY HAD ONE BOWL TO THROW...
SHE FELT GELEK HAD A SHOT AT HITTING DEIRDRE AND BLEW IT.
LOOK! IT'S THEM!
BUT, GELEK ISN'T LIKE THAT. HE LIKES EVERYBODY.
BIG WHOOP.

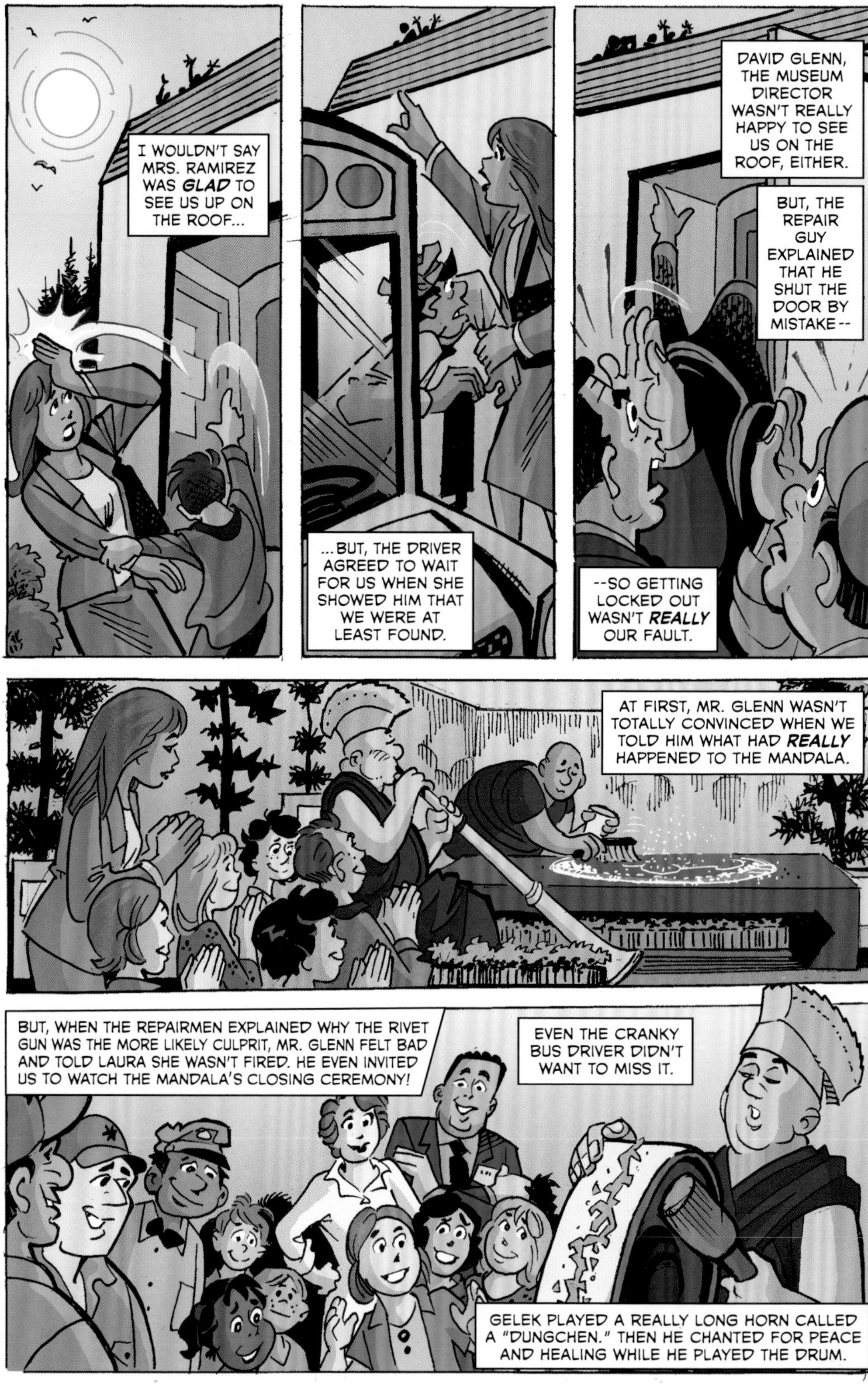
I WOULDN'T SAY MRS. RAMIREZ WAS GLAD TO SEE US UP ON THE ROOF...
...BUT, THE DRIVER AGREED TO WAIT FOR US WHEN SHE SHOWED HIM THAT WE WERE AT LEAST FOUND.
DAVID GLENN, THE MUSEUM DIRECTOR WASN'T REALLY HAPPY TO SEE US ON THE ROOF, EITHER.
BUT, THE REPAIR GUY EXPLAINED THAT HE SHUT THE DOOR BY MISTAKE--
--SO GETTING LOCKED OUT WASN'T REALLY OUR FAULT.
AT FIRST, MR. GLENN WASN'T TOTALLY CONVINCED WHEN WE TOLD HIM WHAT HAD REALLY HAPPENED TO THE MANDALA.
BUT, WHEN THE REPAIRMEN EXPLAINED WHY THE RIVET GUN WAS THE MORE LIKELY CULPRIT, MR. GLENN FELT BAD AND TOLD LAURA SHE WASN'T FIRED. HE EVEN INVITED US TO WATCH THE MANDALA'S CLOSING CEREMONY!
EVEN THE CRANKY BUS DRIVER DIDN'T WANT TO MISS IT.
GELEK PLAYED A REALLY LONG HORN CALLED A "DUNGCHEN." THEN HE CHANTED FOR PEACE AND HEALING WHILE HE PLAYED THE DRUM.

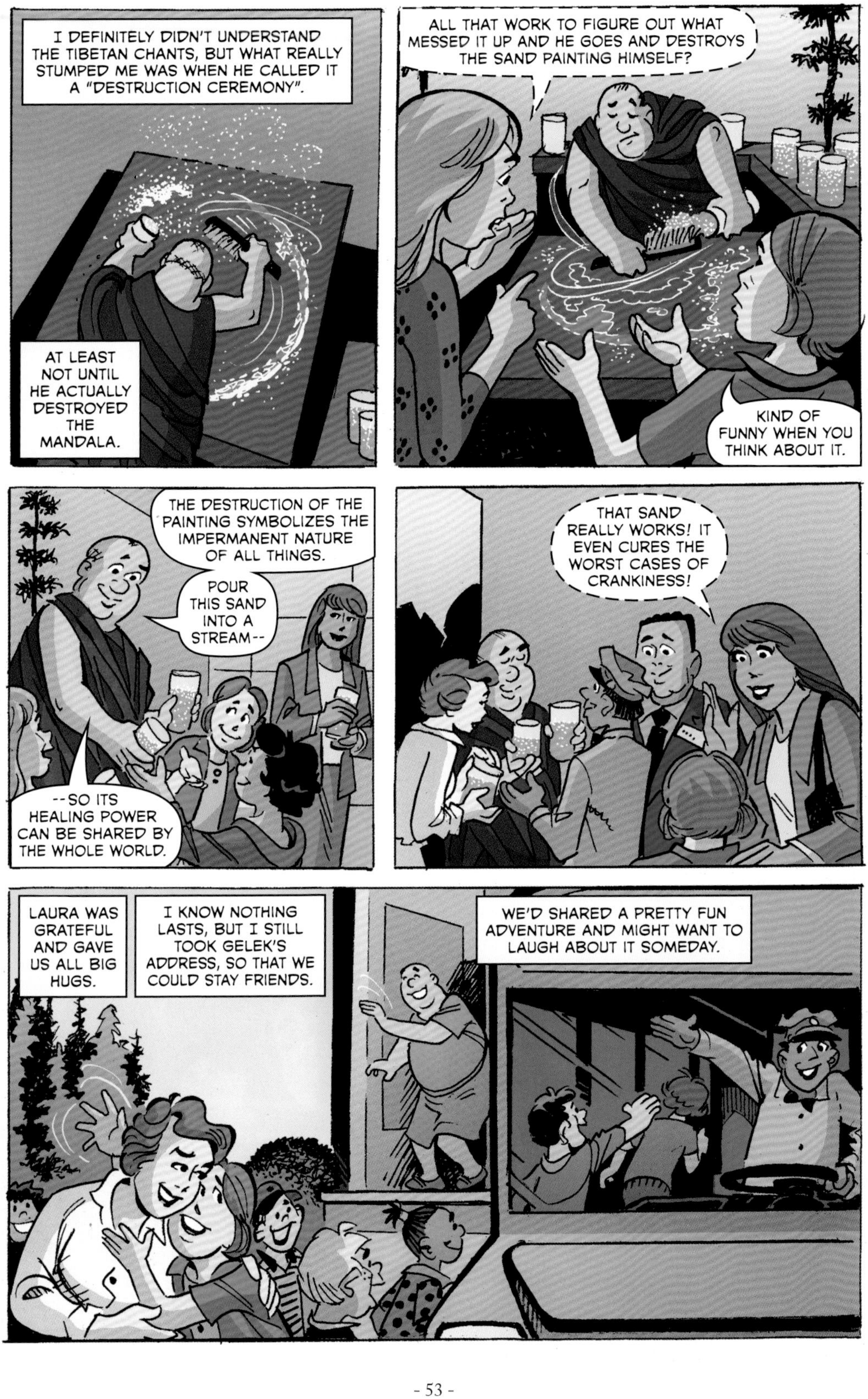
I DEFINITELY DIDN'T UNDERSTAND THE TIBETAN CHANTS, BUT WHAT REALLY STUMPED ME WAS WHEN HE CALLED IT A "DESTRUCTION CEREMONY".
AT LEAST NOT UNTIL HE ACTUALLY DESTROYED THE MANDALA.
ALL THAT WORK TO FIGURE OUT WHAT MESSED IT UP AND HE GOES AND DESTROYS THE SAND PAINTING HIMSELF?
KIND OF FUNNY WHEN YOU THINK ABOUT IT.
THE DESTRUCTION OF THE PAINTING SYMBOLIZES THE IMPERMANENT NATURE OF ALL THINGS.
POUR THIS SAND INTO A STREAM--
--SO ITS HEALING POWER CAN BE SHARED BY THE WHOLE WORLD.
THAT SAND REALLY WORKS! IT EVEN CURES THE WORST CASES OF CRANKINESS!
LAURA WAS GRATEFUL AND GAVE US ALL BIG HUGS.
I KNOW NOTHING LASTS, BUT I STILL TOOK GELEK'S ADDRESS, SO THAT WE COULD STAY FRIENDS.
WE'D SHARED A PRETTY FUN ADVENTURE AND MIGHT WANT TO LAUGH ABOUT IT SOMEDAY.

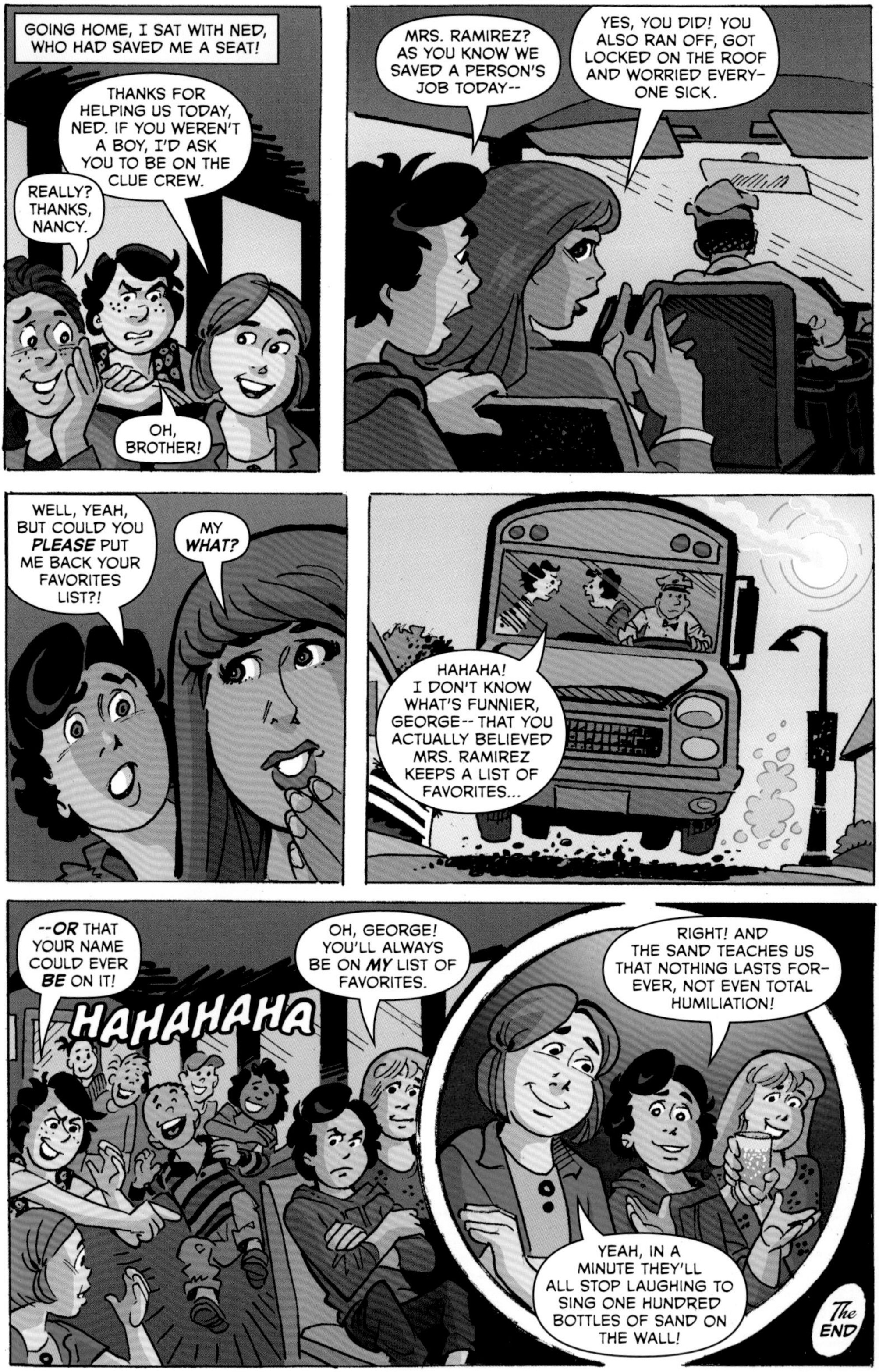
GOING HOME, I SAT WITH NED, WHO HAD SAVED ME A SEAT!
THANKS FOR HELPING US TODAY, NED. IF YOU WEREN'T A BOY, I'D ASK YOU TO BE ON THE CLUE CREW.
REALLY? THANKS, NANCY.
OH, BROTHER!
MRS. RAMIREZ? AS YOU KNOW WE SAVED A PERSON'S JOB TODAY--
YES, YOU DID! YOU ALSO RAN OFF, GOT LOCKED ON THE ROOF AND WORRIED EVERY-ONE SICK.
WELL, YEAH, BUT COULD YOU PLEASE PUT ME BACK YOUR FAVORITES LIST?!
MY WHAT?
HAHAHA! I DON'T KNOW WHAT'S FUNNIER, GEORGE-- THAT YOU ACTUALLY BELIEVED MRS. RAMIREZ KEEPS A LIST OF FAVORITES...
--OR THAT YOUR NAME COULD EVER BE ON IT!
HAHAHAHA
OH, GEORGE! YOU'LL ALWAYS BE ON MY LIST OF FAVORITES.
RIGHT! AND THE SAND TEACHES US THAT NOTHING LASTS FOR-EVER, NOT EVEN TOTAL HUMILIATION!
YEAH, IN A MINUTE THEY'LL ALL STOP LAUGHING TO SING ONE HUNDRED BOTTLES OF SAND ON THE WALL!
The END

NANCY DREW GRAPHIC NOVELS AVAILABLE FROM PAPERCUTZ

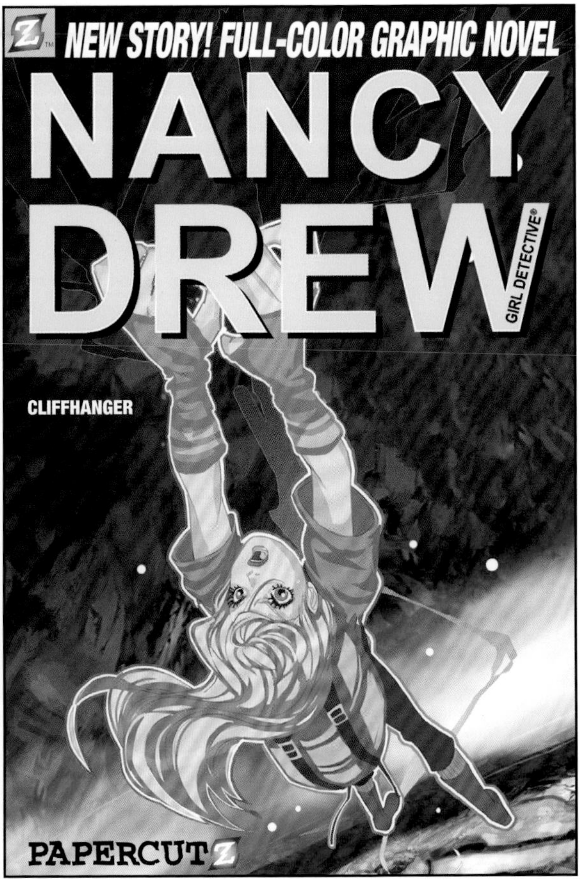
NEW STORY! FULL-COLOR GRAPHIC NOVEL
NANCY DREW
GIRL DETECTIVE®
CLIFFHANGER
PAPERCUTZ

#19 "Cliffhanger"

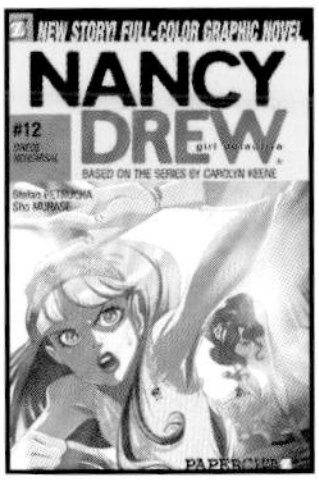
NEW STORY! FULL-COLOR GRAPHIC NOVEL
NANCY DREW
BASED ON THE SERIES BY CAROLYN KEENE

#12 "Dress Reversal"

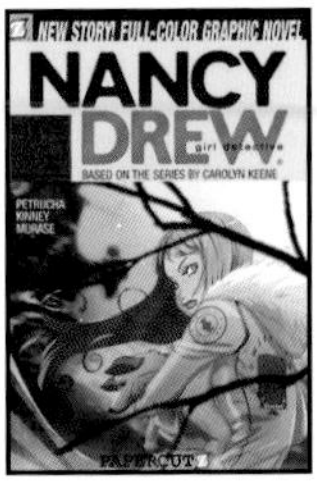
NEW STORY! FULL-COLOR GRAPHIC NOVEL
NANCY DREW
BASED ON THE SERIES BY CAROLYN KEENE

#13 "Doggone Town"

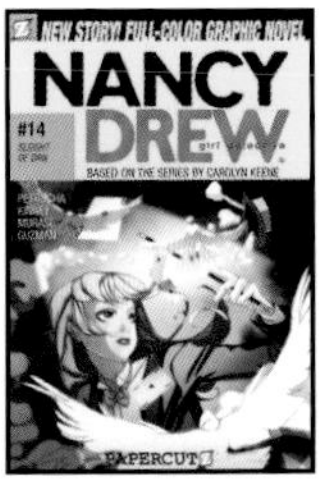
NEW STORY! FULL-COLOR GRAPHIC NOVEL
NANCY DREW
BASED ON THE SERIES BY CAROLYN KEENE

#14 "Sleight of Dan"

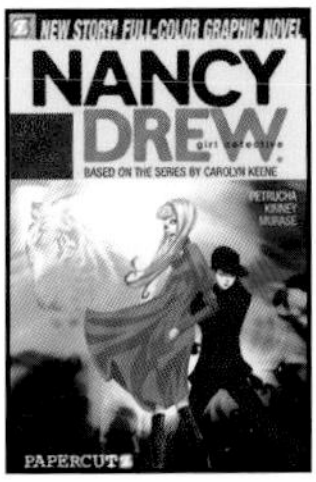
NEW STORY! FULL-COLOR GRAPHIC NOVEL
NANCY DREW
BASED ON THE SERIES BY CAROLYN KEENE

#15 "Tiger Counter"

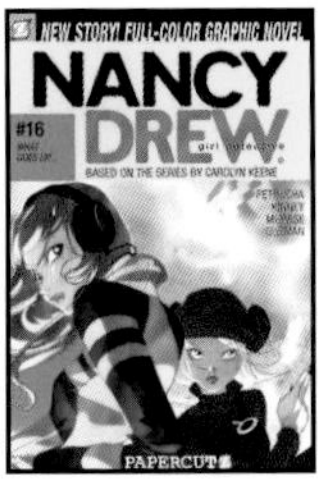
NEW STORY! FULL-COLOR GRAPHIC NOVEL
NANCY DREW
BASED ON THE SERIES BY CAROLYN KEENE

#16 "What Goes Up..."

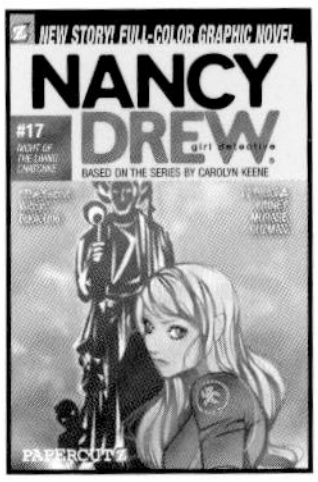
NEW STORY! FULL-COLOR GRAPHIC NOVEL
NANCY DREW
BASED ON THE SERIES BY CAROLYN KEENE

#17 "Night of the Living Chatchke"

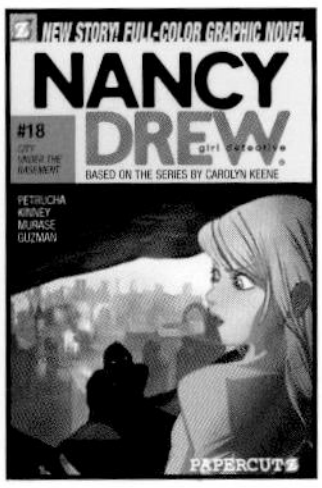
NEW STORY! FULL-COLOR GRAPHIC NOVEL
NANCY DREW
BASED ON THE SERIES BY CAROLYN KEENE

#18 "City Under the Basement"

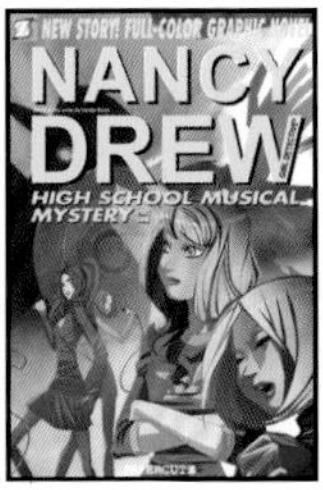
NANCY DREW
HIGH SCHOOL MUSICAL MYSTERY

#20 "High School Musical Mystery" 1

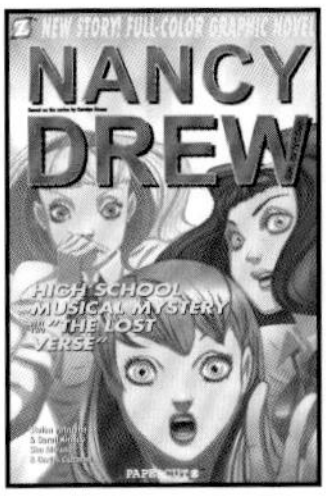
NEW STORY! FULL-COLOR GRAPHIC NOVEL
NANCY DREW

#21 "High School Musical Mystery" 2

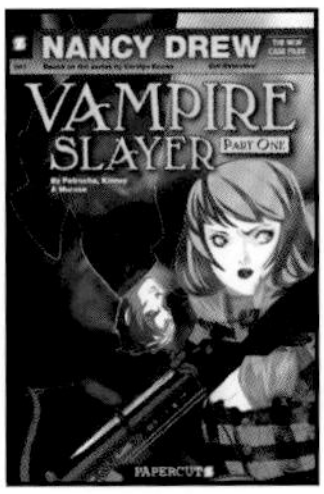
NANCY DREW
VAMPIRE SLAYER PART ONE

The New Case Files #1 "Vampire Slayer" Part 1

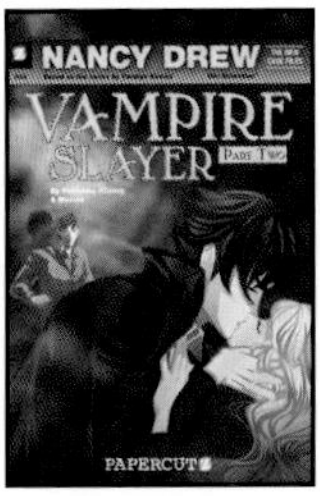
NANCY DREW
VAMPIRE SLAYER PART TWO

The New Case Files #2 "Vampire Slayer" Part 2

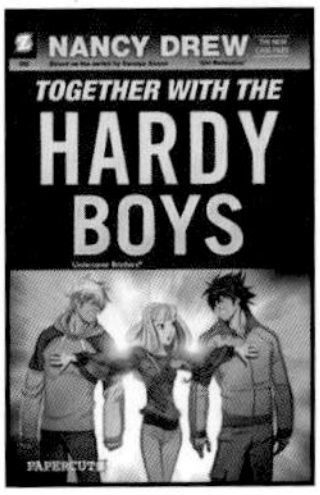
NANCY DREW
TOGETHER WITH THE
HARDY BOYS

The New Case Files #3 "Together with The Hardy Boys"

NANCY DREW graphic novels are available at booksellers everywhere.

NANCY DREW graphic novels #12 – 19 are $7.95 each in paperback and $12.95 each in hardcover, Graphic Novels #20 and #21 are $8.99 each in paperback and $13.99 each in hardcover. NANCY DREW The New Case Files graphic novels are $6.99 each in paperback, and $10.99 each in hardcover. You can also order online at www.papercutz.com. Or call 1-800-886-1223, Monday through Fridays, 9 – 5 EST. MC, Visa, and AmEx accepted. To order by mail, please add $4.00 for postage and handling for first book ordered, $1.00 for each additional book and make check payable to NBM Publishing. Send to: Papercutz, 160 Broadway, Suite 700, East Wing, New York, NY 10038.

NANCY DREW and NANCY DREW The New Case Files graphic novels are also available digitally wherever e-books are sold.

www.papercutz.com

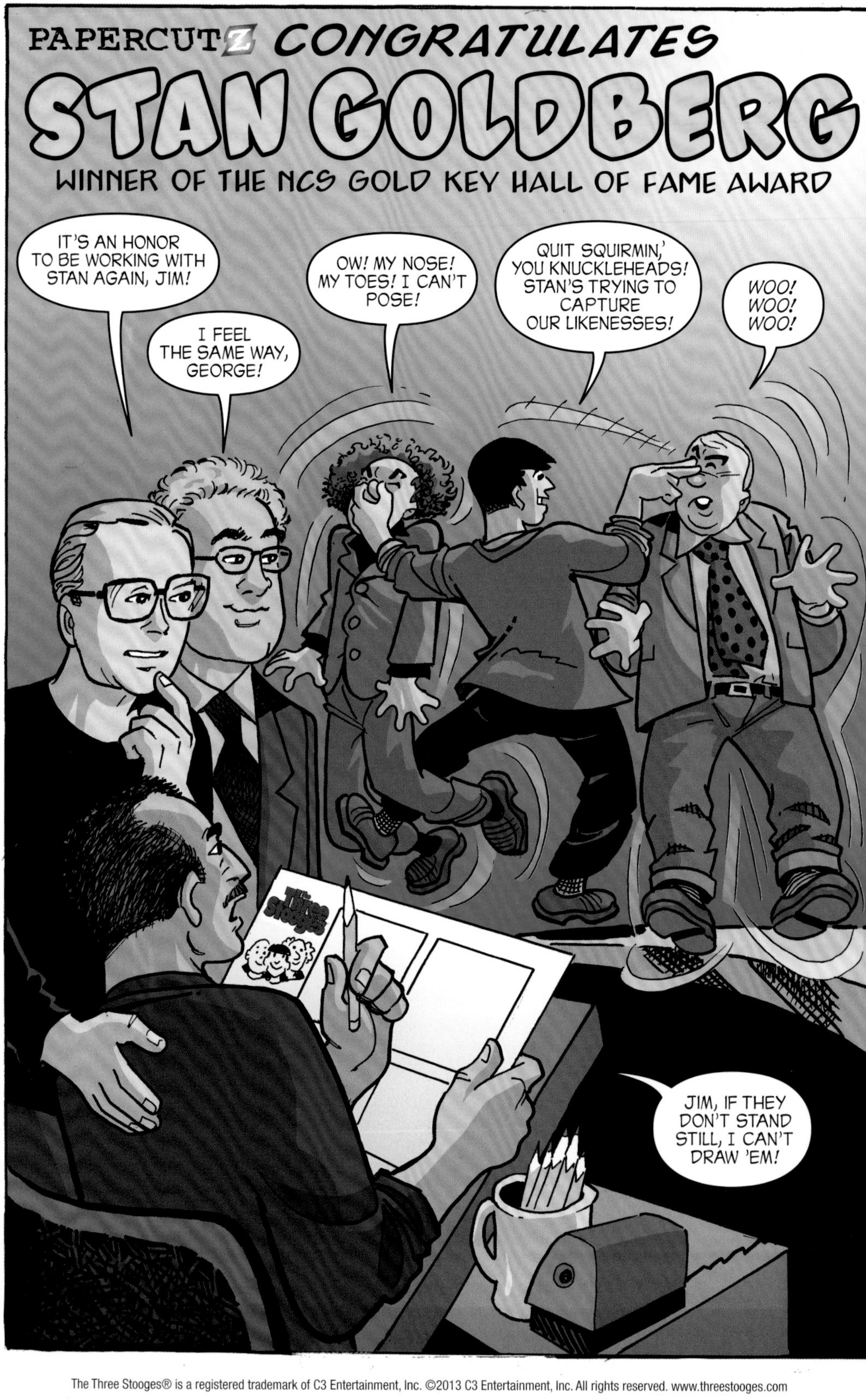
PAPERCUTZ CONGRATULATES
STAN GOLDBERG
WINNER OF THE NCS GOLD KEY HALL OF FAME AWARD
IT'S AN HONOR TO BE WORKING WITH STAN AGAIN, JIM!
I FEEL THE SAME WAY, GEORGE!
OW! MY NOSE! MY TOES! I CAN'T POSE!
QUIT SQUIRMIN,' YOU KNUCKLEHEADS! STAN'S TRYING TO CAPTURE OUR LIKENESSES!
WOO! WOO! WOO!
The Three Stooges
JIM, IF THEY DON'T STAND STILL, I CAN'T DRAW 'EM!

WATCH OUT FOR PAPERCUTZ™

Welcome to the second sleuthy NANCY DREW AND THE CLUE CREW graphic novel by Sarah Kinney and Stan Goldberg from Papercutz, the armchair detectives dedicated to publishing great graphic novels for all ages. I'm Jim Salicrup, Editor-in Chief and erstwhile Baker Street Irregular (adding fiber to my diet cleared that up), here to pontificate and proselytize about Pop Art, but first a few announcements…

Stan Goldberg & Sarah Kinney

After either writing or co-writing virtual every NANCY DREW graphic novel published by Papercutz, our good friend Stefan Petrucha is moving on to other projects such as writing his new series of Hessius Mann novels, teaching an online course on how to writer graphic novels, and writing the POWER RANGERS and PAPERCUTZ SLICES. We of course wish Stefan all the best, and are excited to see what Sarah Kinney's got in store for us all!

Actually, Stefan even wrote a story for THE THREE STOOGES #2 graphic novel, also from Papercutz, illustrated by Stan Goldberg. Stan recently won the Gold Key Hall of Fame award from the National Cartoonists Society, and to celebrate the pin-up on the opposite page was created. We thought Stan's NANCY DREW fans would love to see it too, so there it is! That's me with award-winning writer, George Gladir, by Stan's side, and Moe, Larry, and Curly posing for Mr. G! Congratulations, Stan!

And now for my serious editorializing… Ever since Pop Art appeared in the early 60s, its been a subject of both parody and outright scorn. Being a lifetime fan of comics, I'm a little sensitive about entire forms of art being so casually dismissed. Believe it or not, comics were actually once ridiculed or not taken seriously either (I know, right?). Comics were also seen as totally ephemeral, something to be thrown away when you were done with them. But just like the sand paintings created by Venerable Gelek, comic art is clearly of value. So, while I'm often critical of Pop Art being presented in such a manner, here I am editing a graphic novel that perpetuates the same point of view. But I'm not going to worry about it. Comic art and Pop Art have existed side-by-side for over half a century in an uneasy alliance. Many of the early Pop Art paintings were inspired by panels from old comicbooks. Famed Pop Artist Roy Lichtenstein even did a painting based on a comicbook panel by Stan Goldberg, and I once featured Roy Lichtenstein, with his blessing, in an issue of Marvel's WEB OF SPIDER-MAN. I could go on and on, but instead I'll just say, that when it comes to any form of art, try to always have an open mind. Who knows, you may discover something wonderful.

And speaking of wonderful, check out the special preview of ERNEST & REBECCA #4 "The Land of Walking Stones" by writer Guillaume Bianco and artist Antonello Dalena on the following pages—it's a beautiful example of how comics can be art! And coming soon, NANCY DREW AND THE CLUE CREW #3 "Enter the Dragon Mystery" by Sarah K. and Stan G. You won't want to miss that either!

Jim

STAY IN TOUCH!

EMAIL: salicrup@papercutz.com
WEB: www.papercutz.com
TWITTER: @papercutzgn
FACEBOOK: PAPERCUTZGRAPHICNOVELS
SNAIL MAIL: Papercutz, 160 Broadway, Suite 700, East Wing, New York, NY 10038

Special preview of ERNEST & REBECCA #4 "The Land of Walking Stones"

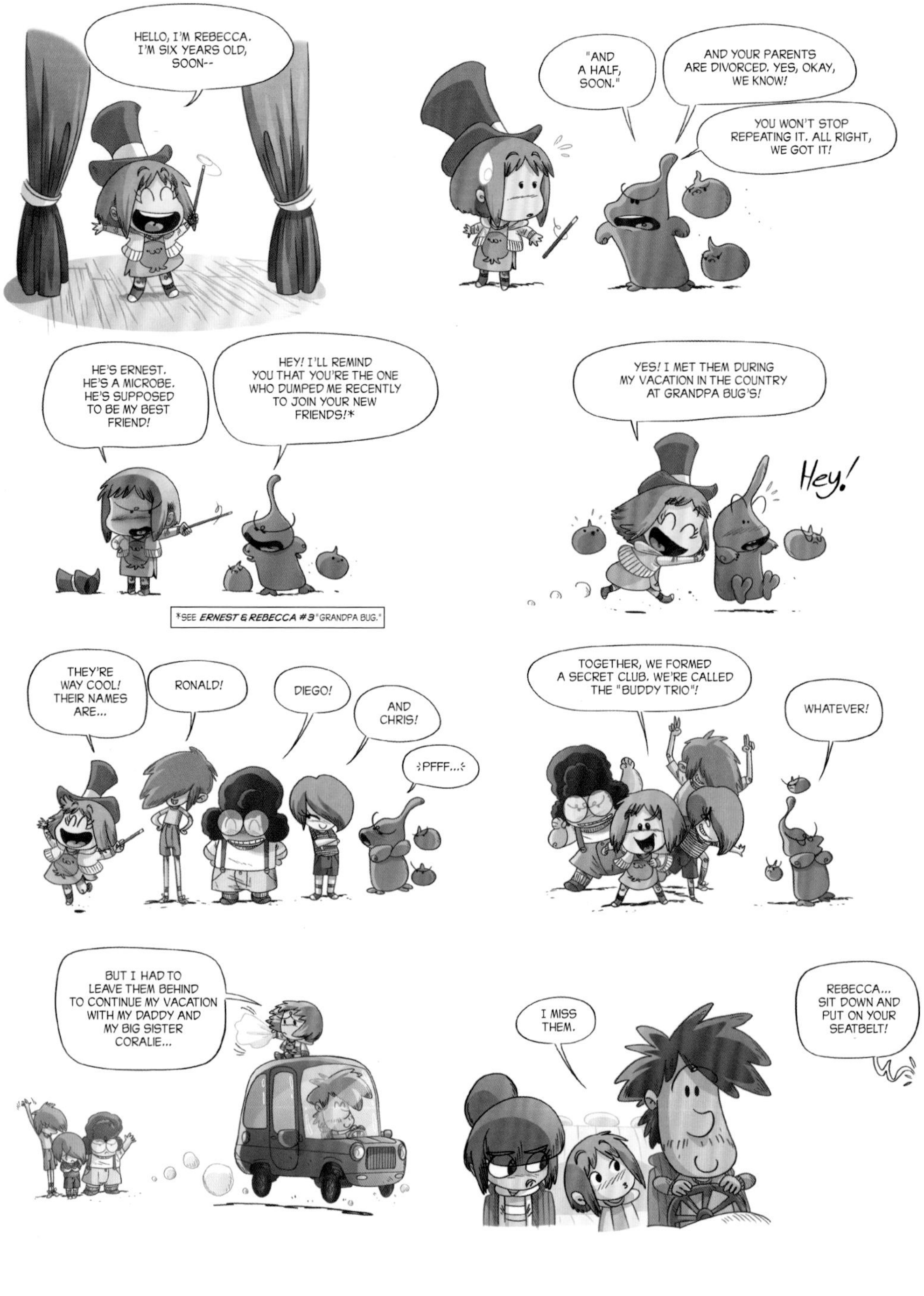
HELLO, I'M REBECCA. I'M SIX YEARS OLD, SOON--
"AND A HALF, SOON."
AND YOUR PARENTS ARE DIVORCED. YES, OKAY, WE KNOW!
YOU WON'T STOP REPEATING IT. ALL RIGHT, WE GOT IT!
HE'S ERNEST. HE'S A MICROBE. HE'S SUPPOSED TO BE MY BEST FRIEND!
HEY! I'LL REMIND YOU THAT YOU'RE THE ONE WHO DUMPED ME RECENTLY TO JOIN YOUR NEW FRIENDS!*
*SEE ERNEST & REBECCA #3 "GRANDPA BUG."
YES! I MET THEM DURING MY VACATION IN THE COUNTRY AT GRANDPA BUG'S!
Hey!
THEY'RE WAY COOL! THEIR NAMES ARE...
RONALD!
DIEGO!
AND CHRIS!
PFFF...
TOGETHER, WE FORMED A SECRET CLUB. WE'RE CALLED THE "BUDDY TRIO"!
WHATEVER!
BUT I HAD TO LEAVE THEM BEHIND TO CONTINUE MY VACATION WITH MY DADDY AND MY BIG SISTER CORALIE...
I MISS THEM.
REBECCA... SIT DOWN AND PUT ON YOUR SEATBELT!

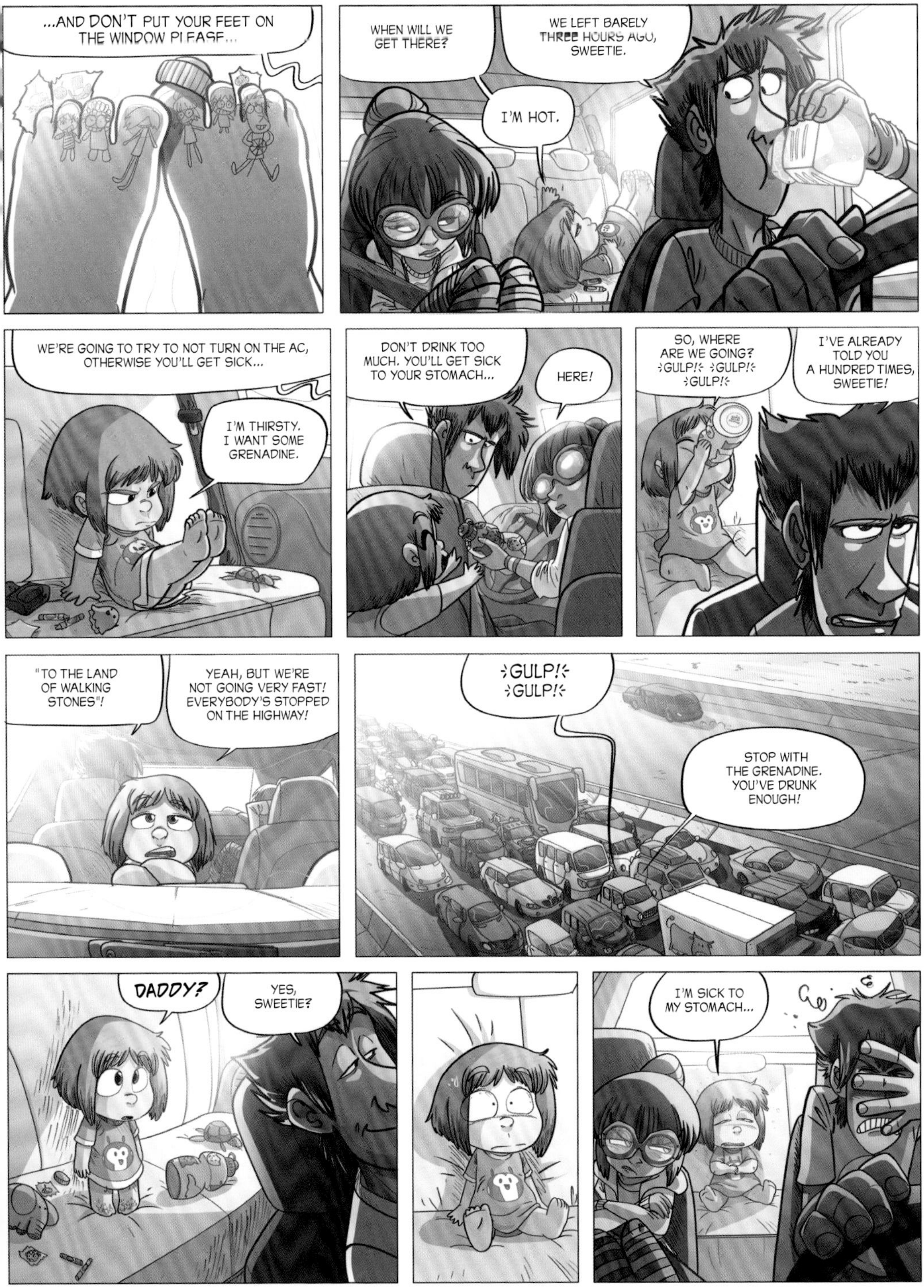
...AND DON'T PUT YOUR FEET ON THE WINDOW PLEASE...
WHEN WILL WE GET THERE?
WE LEFT BARELY THREE HOURS AGO, SWEETIE.
I'M HOT.
WE'RE GOING TO TRY TO NOT TURN ON THE AC, OTHERWISE YOU'LL GET SICK...
I'M THIRSTY. I WANT SOME GRENADINE.
DON'T DRINK TOO MUCH. YOU'LL GET SICK TO YOUR STOMACH...
HERE!
SO, WHERE ARE WE GOING? GULP! GULP! GULP!
I'VE ALREADY TOLD YOU A HUNDRED TIMES, SWEETIE!
"TO THE LAND OF WALKING STONES"!
YEAH, BUT WE'RE NOT GOING VERY FAST! EVERYBODY'S STOPPED ON THE HIGHWAY!
GULP! GULP!
STOP WITH THE GRENADINE. YOU'VE DRUNK ENOUGH!
DADDY?
YES, SWEETIE?
I'M SICK TO MY STOMACH...

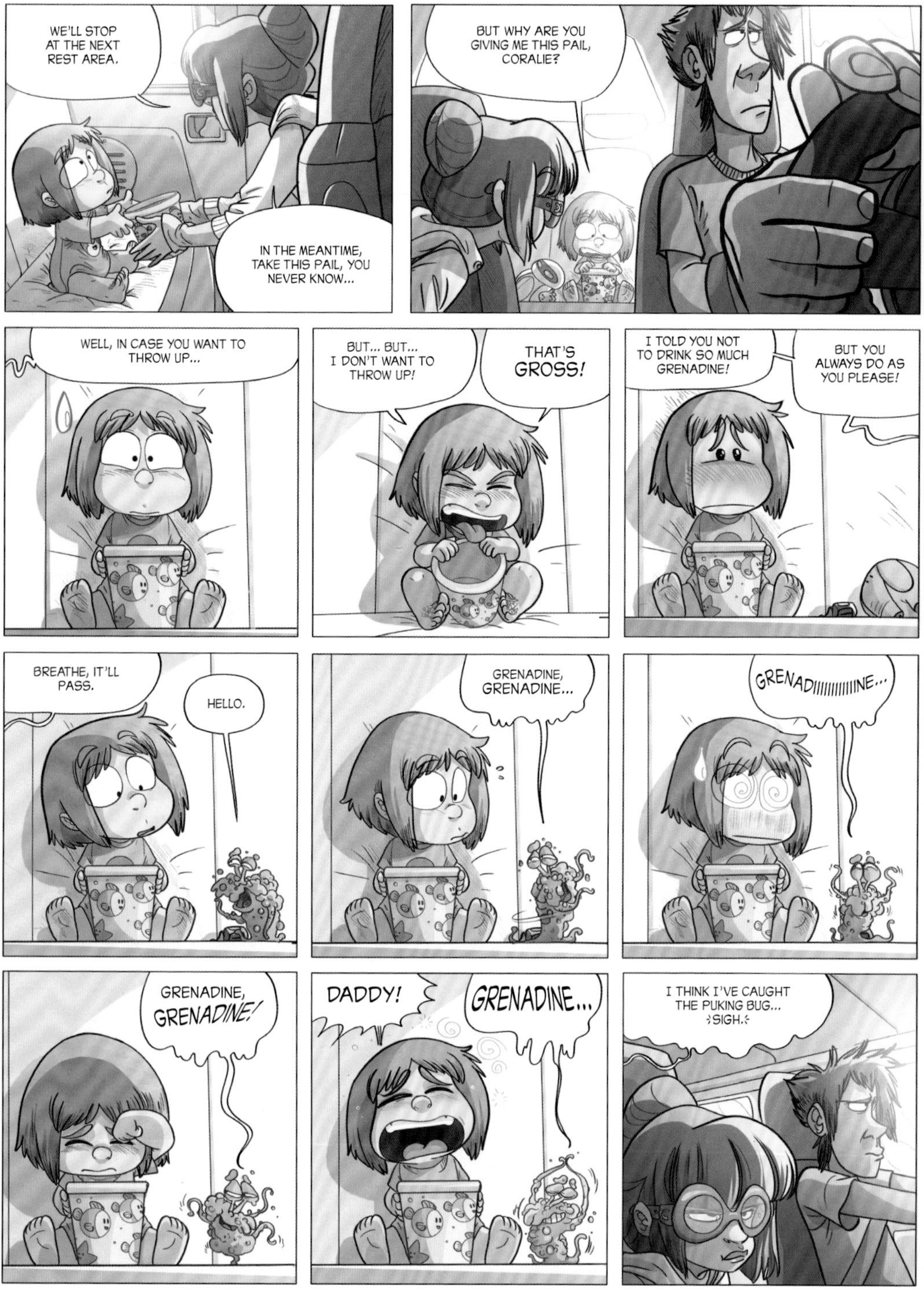
WE'LL STOP AT THE NEXT REST AREA.
IN THE MEANTIME, TAKE THIS PAIL, YOU NEVER KNOW...
BUT WHY ARE YOU GIVING ME THIS PAIL, CORALIE?
WELL, IN CASE YOU WANT TO THROW UP...
BUT... BUT... I DON'T WANT TO THROW UP!
THAT'S GROSS!
I TOLD YOU NOT TO DRINK SO MUCH GRENADINE!
BUT YOU ALWAYS DO AS YOU PLEASE!
BREATHE, IT'LL PASS.
HELLO.
GRENADINE, GRENADINE...
GRENADIIIIIIIIIIIINE...
GRENADINE, GRENADINE!
DADDY!
GRENADINE...
I THINK I'VE CAUGHT THE PUKING BUG... ⊰SIGH.⊱

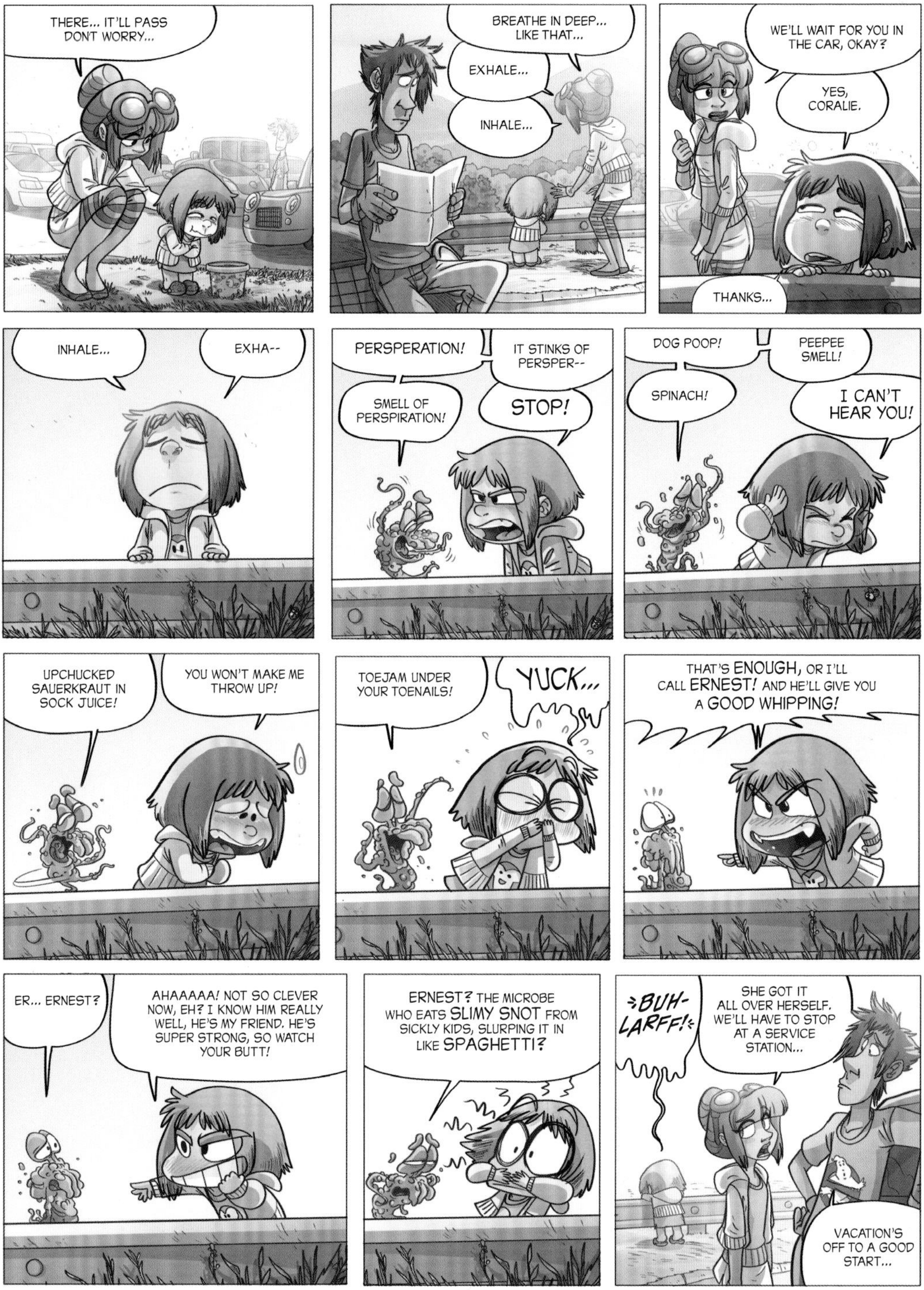
THERE... IT'LL PASS DON'T WORRY...
BREATHE IN DEEP... LIKE THAT...
EXHALE...
INHALE...
WE'LL WAIT FOR YOU IN THE CAR, OKAY?
YES, CORALIE.
THANKS...
INHALE...
EXHA--
PERSPERATION!
IT STINKS OF PERSPER--
SMELL OF PERSPIRATION!
STOP!
DOG POOP!
PEEPEE SMELL!
SPINACH!
I CAN'T HEAR YOU!
UPCHUCKED SAUERKRAUT IN SOCK JUICE!
YOU WON'T MAKE ME THROW UP!
TOEJAM UNDER YOUR TOENAILS!
YUCK...
THAT'S ENOUGH, OR I'LL CALL ERNEST! AND HE'LL GIVE YOU A GOOD WHIPPING!
ER... ERNEST?
AHAAAAAA! NOT SO CLEVER NOW, EH? I KNOW HIM REALLY WELL, HE'S MY FRIEND. HE'S SUPER STRONG, SO WATCH YOUR BUTT!
ERNEST? THE MICROBE WHO EATS SLIMY SNOT FROM SICKLY KIDS, SLURPING IT IN LIKE SPAGHETTI?
BUH-LARFF!
SHE GOT IT ALL OVER HERSELF. WE'LL HAVE TO STOP AT A SERVICE STATION...
VACATION'S OFF TO A GOOD START...

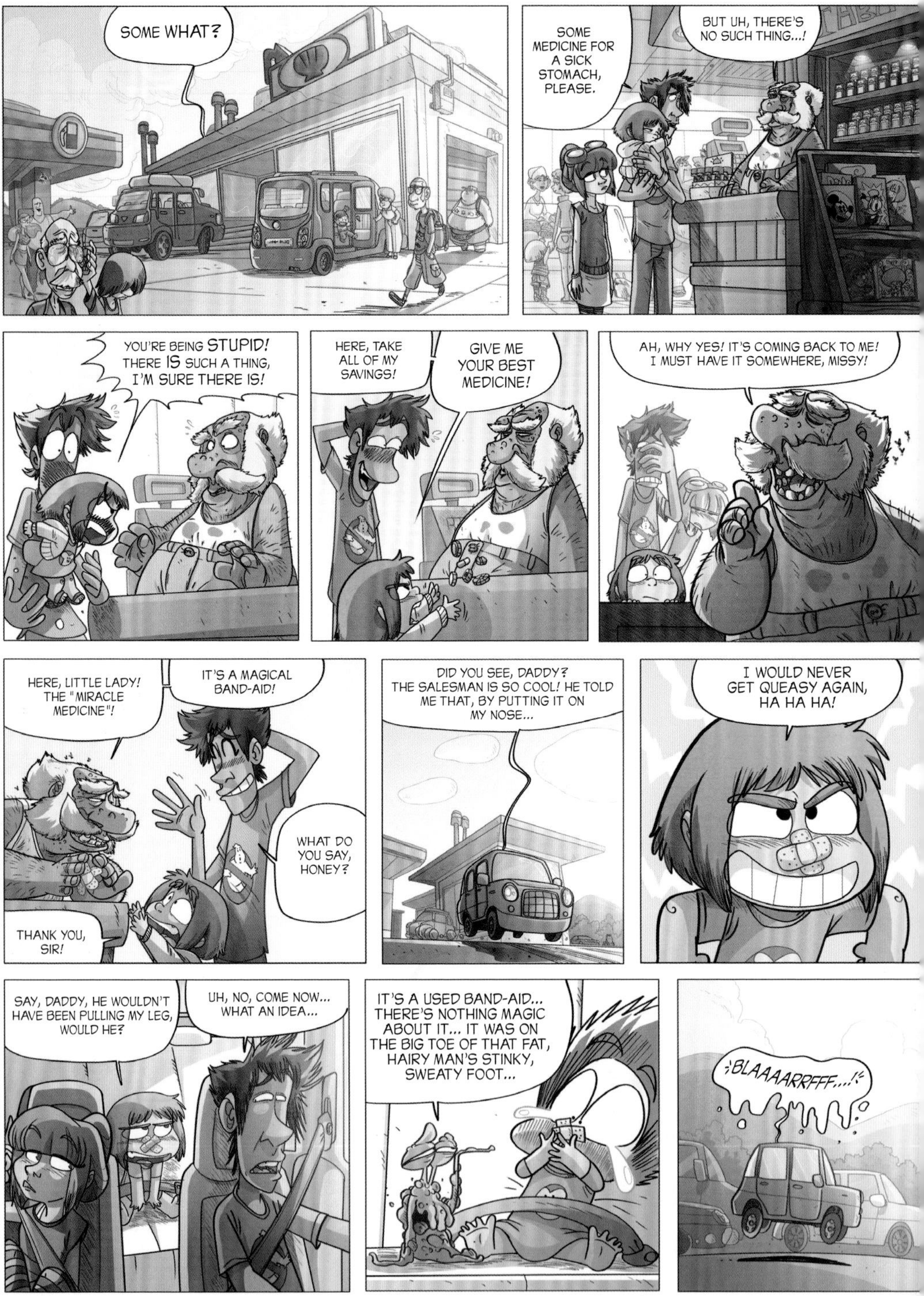
SOME WHAT?
SOME MEDICINE FOR A SICK STOMACH, PLEASE.
BUT UH, THERE'S NO SUCH THING...!
YOU'RE BEING STUPID! THERE IS SUCH A THING, I'M SURE THERE IS!
HERE, TAKE ALL OF MY SAVINGS!
GIVE ME YOUR BEST MEDICINE!
AH, WHY YES! IT'S COMING BACK TO ME! I MUST HAVE IT SOMEWHERE, MISSY!
HERE, LITTLE LADY! THE "MIRACLE MEDICINE"!
IT'S A MAGICAL BAND-AID!
WHAT DO YOU SAY, HONEY?
THANK YOU, SIR!
DID YOU SEE, DADDY? THE SALESMAN IS SO COOL! HE TOLD ME THAT, BY PUTTING IT ON MY NOSE...
I WOULD NEVER GET QUEASY AGAIN, HA HA HA!
SAY, DADDY, HE WOULDN'T HAVE BEEN PULLING MY LEG, WOULD HE?
UH, NO, COME NOW... WHAT AN IDEA...
IT'S A USED BAND-AID... THERE'S NOTHING MAGIC ABOUT IT... IT WAS ON THE BIG TOE OF THAT FAT, HAIRY MAN'S STINKY, SWEATY FOOT...
¡BLAAAARRFFF...!

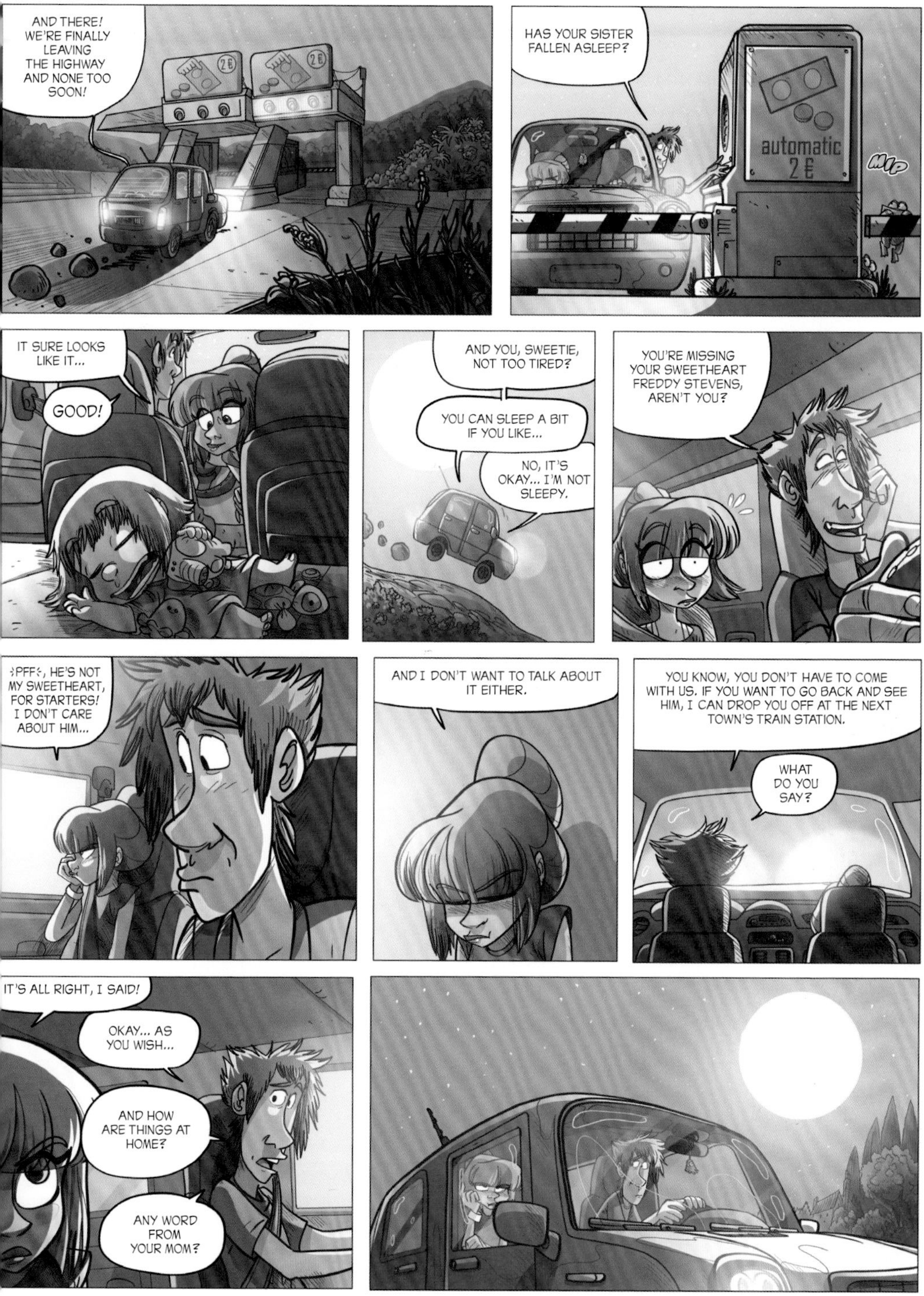
AND THERE! WE'RE FINALLY LEAVING THE HIGHWAY AND NONE TOO SOON!
2 €
2 €
HAS YOUR SISTER FALLEN ASLEEP?
automatic 2 €
MIP
IT SURE LOOKS LIKE IT...
GOOD!
AND YOU, SWEETIE, NOT TOO TIRED?
YOU CAN SLEEP A BIT IF YOU LIKE...
NO, IT'S OKAY... I'M NOT SLEEPY.
YOU'RE MISSING YOUR SWEETHEART FREDDY STEVENS, AREN'T YOU?
PFF, HE'S NOT MY SWEETHEART, FOR STARTERS! I DON'T CARE ABOUT HIM...
AND I DON'T WANT TO TALK ABOUT IT EITHER.
YOU KNOW, YOU DON'T HAVE TO COME WITH US. IF YOU WANT TO GO BACK AND SEE HIM, I CAN DROP YOU OFF AT THE NEXT TOWN'S TRAIN STATION.
WHAT DO YOU SAY?
IT'S ALL RIGHT, I SAID!
OKAY... AS YOU WISH...
AND HOW ARE THINGS AT HOME?
ANY WORD FROM YOUR MOM?

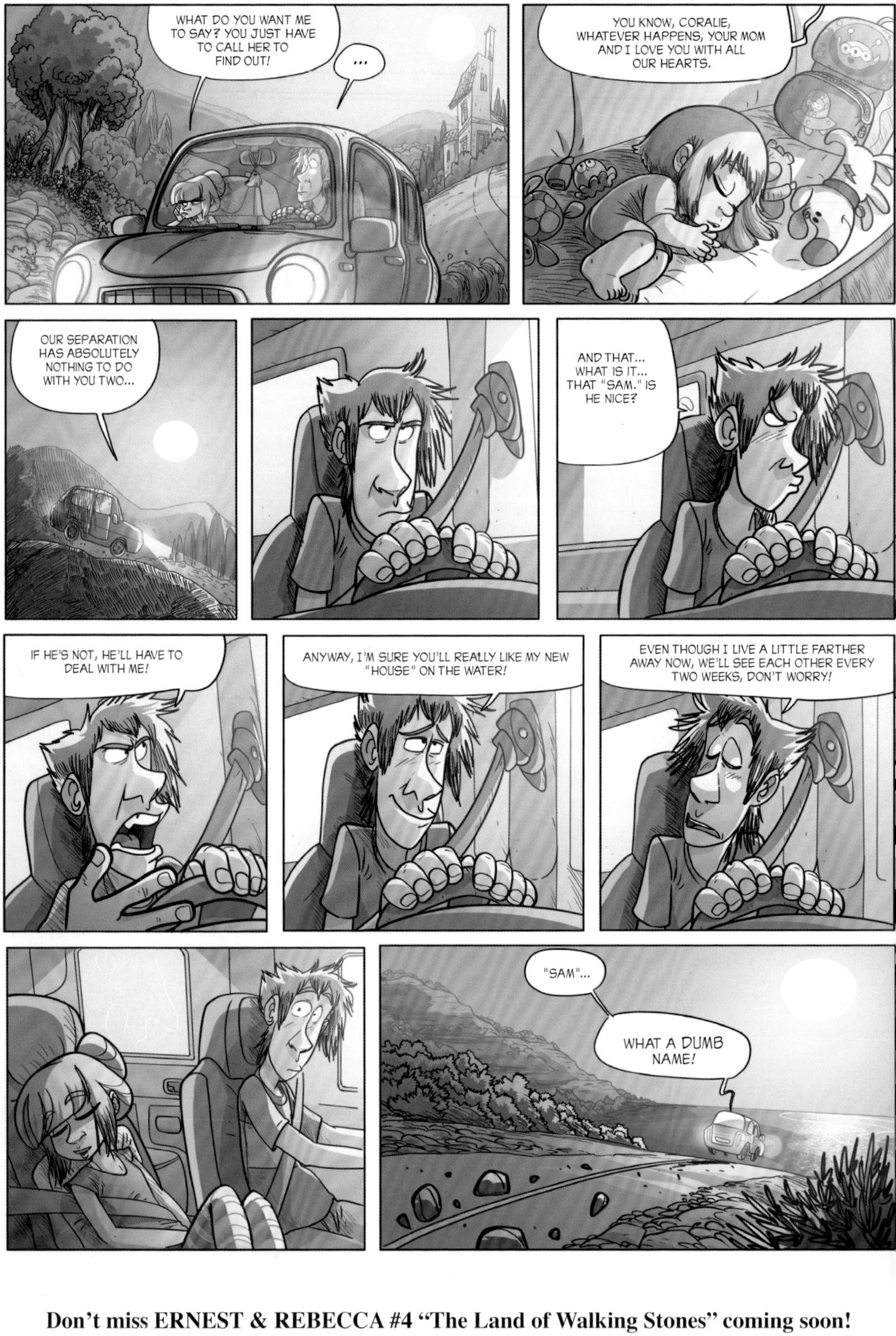
WHAT DO YOU WANT ME TO SAY? YOU JUST HAVE TO CALL HER TO FIND OUT!
...
YOU KNOW, CORALIE, WHATEVER HAPPENS, YOUR MOM AND I LOVE YOU WITH ALL OUR HEARTS.
OUR SEPARATION HAS ABSOLUTELY NOTHING TO DO WITH YOU TWO...
AND THAT... WHAT IS IT... THAT "SAM." IS HE NICE?
IF HE'S NOT, HE'LL HAVE TO DEAL WITH ME!
ANYWAY, I'M SURE YOU'LL REALLY LIKE MY NEW "HOUSE" ON THE WATER!
EVEN THOUGH I LIVE A LITTLE FARTHER AWAY NOW, WE'LL SEE EACH OTHER EVERY TWO WEEKS, DON'T WORRY!
"SAM"...
WHAT A DUMB NAME!

Don't miss ERNEST & REBECCA #4 "The Land of Walking Stones" coming soon!